Ghosthunters

and the

Totally

Moldy

Baroness!

Ghosthunters

and the

Totally

Moldy

Baroness!

by **CORNELIA FUNKE**

Chicken House

SCHOLASTIC INC./NEW YORK

First published in Germany as *Gespensterjäger in der Gruselburg* by Loewe Verlag

Original text copyright © 1995 by Loewe Verlag

English translation by Helena Ragg-Kirkby copyright © 2007 by Cornelia Funke

Published in the United Kingdom in 2007 by The Chicken House,

2 Palmer Street, Frome, Somerset BA11 1DS.

www.doublecluck.com

Interior illustrations copyright © 2007 by Cornelia Funke

Library of Congress Cataloging-in-Publication Data Available

ISBN-13: 978-0-439-86266-0

ISBN-10: 0-439-86266-3

10 9 8 7 6 5 4 3 2 1   07 08 09 10 11

Printed in the U.S.A.   23

First American edition, January 2007

The text type was set in Berthold Baskerville Book.

The display type was set in P22 Kane, Mister Frisky, and Zsazsa Galore.

Book design by Leyah Jensen

For
Elmar
and
Gitta

WHEN SANTA FELL TO EARTH

GHOSTHUNTERS
and the Incredibly Revolting Ghost!

GHOSTHUNTERS
and the Gruesome Invincible Lightning Ghost!

CONTENTS

TOM   HUGO the ASG   HETTY

Let me introduce three of the most successful ghosthunters of our time.

Here (from right to left) are **Hetty Hyssop, Hugo the ASG,** and **Tom**.

You might not be able to tell by looking at them, but they are one of the best ghosthunting teams in the entire world.

Hetty Hyssop has under her belt more than fifty years' professional experience in the field.

Tom, her human assistant, is just about to take his **SGHD** (**S**econd **G**host**H**unting **D**iploma).

And Hugo the ASG – well, his help is, of course, quite invaluable, because as an ASG (**A**veragely **S**pooky **G**host) he has extensive insider knowledge at his disposal.

But enough of this introductory talk! Read on for an adventure in which only the desperate courage of our ghosthunters can save them! For this time, Hyssop & Co. have to deal with one of the most terrible – not to mention terribly moldy! – inhabitants of the ghost world. . . .

A Cry for Help

One February afternoon, the fax machine of the famous ghosthunter Hetty Hyssop spat out the following message:

My dear Mrs. Hyssop,

My name is Theodore Worm and neither I nor my dear wife, Amelia, are easily scared. Over the last few days, however, we have both experienced incidents that have devastated both our nerves and our health. A week ago my wife and I took over the management of Gloomsburg Castle, an estate belonging to the von Gloomstones. When we arrived, we heard rumors that a ghost had been up to mischief at the castle for years. Our employers never mentioned it, though, and so we initially ignored the gossip. After all, we ARE living in the twenty-first century!

Since our arrival, however, we have witnessed such a number of puzzling and deeply disturbing incidents that we are gradually starting to doubt our sanity. Your company, Hyssop & Co., was recommended to us by OFFCOCAG (the OFFice for Combating CAstle Ghosts). Please help us! We are desperate!

Yours sincerely (and deeply distraught),

Theodore and Amelia Worm

It wasn't much to go on, but the three ghosthunters at Hyssop & Co. were well used to such a lack of detail in the calls for help from their terrified clients. After several failed attempts to speak to the Worms on the phone, the trio loaded their car with their basic ghost-hunting equipment, added a couple of special devices for fighting off historical ghosts, and packed Tom's brand-new computer, which enabled him to tap into the extensive data bank of **RICOG** (the **R**esearch **I**nstitute for **CO**mbating **G**hosts). Then they set off for Gloomsburg Castle without further delay.

It was a cold, gray winter's day and the rain was pelting down on the pavement as Hetty Hyssop drove her old station wagon into the little village of Gloomstone.

"Well, I can't see any castle," said Tom, pressing his nose against the steamed-up car window. "Just a church, two banks, and a takeout place. Not even a sign saying 'this way to the castle' or anything."

"Right," said Hetty Hyssop, stopping by the curb. "Then we'll just have to ask. Hugo, make yourself scarce."

"OOOOOOK," breathed Hugo, and disappeared underneath the backseat, while Hetty Hyssop wound down her window.

"Excuse me!" she called out to a man rushing past with a sopping-wet dachshund on a leash. "We're looking for Baron von Gloomstone's castle."

The man almost trod on his dachshund in horror. He swallowed, looked around, leaned closer to Hetty Hyssop, and whispered, "What do you want with *that* place?"

"Oh, I've got some business there," Hetty Hyssop answered.

"Jeepers creepers, have you got a death wish?" hissed the man. "Turn around and drive straight back home while you still have all your marbles intact!"

"Thanks very much for your advice," said Hetty Hyssop, "but you needn't worry about my marbles. I'd just like to know the way. So can you help me?"

The man shrugged his shoulders and pointed down the road.

"First right, second left, then straight on until . . ."

He stared past Hetty Hyssop, his mouth open.

"Straight on until?" asked Hetty Hyssop. "Until where?"

"There!" breathed the man, pointing at the white fingers gently lifting Hetty's hat up into the air. His dachshund threw back its head and howled.

"That? Oh, that's nothing!" Hetty Hyssop gave

Hugo's wobbly fingers an irritated slap. "Straight on until where, then?"

But the man couldn't utter another single sound. He stood there with his mouth open whilst his dog wound its leash around his legs.

"Until whhhhhhere?" breathed Hugo, blowing his moldy breath into the poor man's face. "Come on, spit it ooooout, or Iiiiii'll tickle yoooooou, got it?"

"S – s – straight a – a – ahead u – u – until you get to the bu – bu – bus stop, then t – t – take the track across the field," the dachshund owner burst out.

"Thanks," said Hetty Hyssop. Then she hastily wound up the window and put her foot down on the gas pedal.

The poor man was left standing in the rain staring after them, completely befuddled.

"Ha-ha-ha-ha-ha!" howled Hugo, waving through the back window. "Ha-ha-ha-ha-ha, just looook at him!"

"Hey, have you gone nuts?" Tom snapped. "Can't you give these stupid ghostly jokes a rest for once?"

"Fog," said Hetty Hyssop. She rounded the next corner, tires squealing. "That ASG has a head full of fog. First right, second left. Tom, can you see the bus stop anywhere?"

5

"Ungraaaaateful," grumbled Hugo. "Yooooooou're soooo ungraaaaateful."

"Oh, be quiet, you're getting on my nerves," said Tom. "I just hope you don't act like that once we're in the castle. There!" He wiped the misted-up window with his sleeve. "The bus stop's over there – and here's the trail, where that broken signpost is."

Hetty Hyssop's car bumped its way down the muddy trail, with Hugo wobbling around on the back-seat like a bright green bowl of jelly.

"I feeeeeel sick!" he moaned. "I feeeeel sooo sick!"

"Serves you right," said Tom, and caught his breath. "Oh my goodness!" he murmured.

Gloomsburg Castle lay before them.

It squatted there, large and gray, surrounded by a black moat that reflected the ivy-covered walls.

"Oh my goodness!" Tom said again.

Hetty Hyssop brought her car to a lurching halt in front of the drawbridge.

The rain dripped down from the gargoyles baring their teeth above the castle door.

"I like it," breathed Hugo. "Iiiii'm not joooooking, I think it reeeeeeally is very niiiiice."

"'Nice' isn't exactly the word I'd use!" Tom fished out his backpack from the backseat, pulled his hood over his head, and opened the car door. Rain lashed him in the face and the wind tore at his jacket. Blinking, Tom threw his head back and looked up at the castle's towers. Their tips were fortified with iron, and they thrust their way into the sky like lances.

"Impressive, isn't it?" Hetty Hyssop fetched their bags of equipment out of the trunk and shoved Tom's computer into his hands. "Come on," she said, and set off decisively for the drawbridge. "We'll fetch the rest of our stuff later."

Tom nodded and looked around for Hugo. But the only trace of the ASG was some shimmering slime on Tom's backpack.

"Hey, Hugo!" Tom shouted, banging on the backpack. "Come out at once. Go sliming around somewhere else, got it?"

"Yoooooou're a meeeeeanie," breathed Hugo, wobbling into broad daylight. "It's tooooo light, much tooooo light! And what abooooout this dreadful wind? It will blow meeeee to pieeeeeeeces."

Tom ignored him. The drawbridge was wet from the rain, and he almost slipped on the well-worn planks

7

as he made a grab for the guardrails before following Hetty Hyssop. Hugo wobbled up behind his shoulders and pointed with one icy finger into the black water that filled the castle moat.

"Iiiii can smell ghoooooosts!" he whispered. "Water Ghosts, Marsh Ghosts, Ancient Ghosts. Yooohooooo!" Giggling with delight, he disappeared through the dark archway in the castle wall.

Tom tore himself away from the sight of the dark water and hastily stumbled after him, past the gargoyles and the holes that had once been used to pour hot pitch onto the heads of unwanted visitors. As he crossed the castle courtyard he suddenly had the feeling of being watched by ancient eyes. Angry eyes, full of hatred and spite.

But when he looked around, there was nothing to be seen.

Hetty Hyssop was already standing with Hugo on the wide staircase that led up to the castle's main entrance. Sopping wet and freezing cold, Tom joined them. Next to the door was a big notice:

GLOOMSBURG CASTLE
Open to the public weekdays from 10 A.M. – 12 P.M.,

Sundays 10 A.M. – 4 P.M.

Guided tours by prior arrangement only.

"Hugo," said Hetty Hyssop, "if you behave with the Worms as you did with the poor dachshund owner, I'll personally throw raw eggs at you. Is that clear?"

"Ooooooh my," moaned Hugo, slumping down into himself. "Not eeeeeeven a little joke or twooooo?"

"Well, you can certainly try," Hetty Hyssop replied, "but for each joke, as I said, there'll be at least one nice dripping raw egg."

Then she pulled the chain that was dangling down next to the huge wooden door, and a bell clanged somewhere within the depths of the castle. . . .

A Ghostly Warning

"**W**ho's there?" whispered a scared voice from behind the big door.

"It's Hyssop and Company," answered Hetty. "The ghosthunters."

"Oh!" The door opened a crack, and a man and a woman peered out anxiously.

"Mr. and Mrs. Worm?" asked Tom. "Hello, may we come in?"

"Hellooooooooo!" breathed Hugo, giving them a friendly wave with his white fingers.

Bang! The door was slammed in their faces.

Hetty Hyssop sighed – and pulled the chain once more.

"That's just my assistant, Hugo the ASG!" cried Hetty. "There's no need to worry; just open the door again."

Animated whispering started up behind the door. Then it opened again.

"Come in," whispered a small, fat woman with a red ribbon nestled in her gray hair.

"Yes, come in," whispered the man. "You must excuse us, but your assistant – um – yes, well, he looks a bit strange."

"He's a ghost," said Tom. "But a perfectly harmless one."

"Hey, Iiiii'm *not* perfectly harmless," breathed Hugo. "Iiiiii'd say . . ." But he piped down when he saw Hetty Hyssop's stern look.

It wasn't much warmer inside the castle than outside. The high, gloomy entrance hall was lit only by a couple of candles flickering in iron holders attached to the soot-blackened walls.

"Oh, we are so glad you've come," whispered Mrs. Worm, her voice trembling. "My saucepans all went flying through the air again today. Flying through the air, I tell you!" She gave a small sob and straightened her ribbon.

"Aha!" Hetty Hyssop nodded and looked around. "Well, I suggest we move as quickly as possible into a well-heated room – because very few ghosts like that – where you can tell us exactly, and without any ghostly interruptions, what's been going on."

"Oh, then we're probably best off in the old armory. My husband's set up a little workshop there," whispered Mrs. Worm. "Come on."

With short, rapid steps she hurried toward a huge stone staircase. The two suits of armor standing at the foot of it had no arms, and one was missing a leg.

"As you can see, everything's in a dreadful state," said Mr. Worm. "Since we've been here, I've been busy with restorations. But I've barely finished something when *whoosh!* It flies through the air, or the most disgusting spots of mud appear on it all of a sudden. It's terrible."

"Mud?" Tom cast a glance at the shimmering trail Hugo had left on the stony floor. "You're sure it's not slime?"

"Slime?" Mrs. Worm shook her head. "Oh, no. It is mud. But, as I said, quite disgusting as well."

Tom exchanged an inquiring look with Hetty Hyssop.

"This way, please!" Mrs. Worm led them from the staircase into a corridor. Between the narrow windows, vast numbers of lances, spiked maces, swords, and other murderous tools hung from the walls.

"That's the Baron's famous weapon collection," whispered Mrs. Worm. "Those lances have already

13

flown past our ears several times. One even followed me to the kitchen! It really is a miracle we've not been skewered yet."

"Very interesting," said Hetty Hyssop. "Oh, and by the way, you don't need to whisper. Most ghosts can't hear particularly well. They smell their victims, which is a highly reliable method in and of itself, unfortunately enough."

"Truuuuue. And . . ." Hugo turned a bluish color. ". . . Iiiii can smell ssssssomething now. Sooooomething old and spitefuuuul!"

Disconcerted, he wobbled a couple of feet backward.

Tom quickly rummaged through his backpack and pulled out a large spray bottle filled with seawater.

"Quick!" cried Hetty Hyssop. "Against the wall!"

Mr. Worm obeyed, but Mrs. Worm stood as if rooted to the spot, staring upward. High on the wall, a gigantic spear was moving against the iron hoops that held it to the wall. Its wooden handle thrashed to and fro like a wooden snake. Tom squirted a full load of salt water onto it and the lance went as limp as a piece of rope, but then two maces freed themselves, flew through the air, and bored their way into the floor. Soon sabers, spears, and lances were all raining

down – and, right in the middle of them, Mrs. Worm began to giggle.

It was a quite repellent giggle, hoarse and hollow.

And then Mrs. Worm's head started to light up like a Halloween jack-o'-lantern. Her face became blurred, as if it were made of liquid. Her eyebrows thickened, green slime dripped from her hair, and her mouth twisted itself into a revolting smile.

"The Baroness!" cried Mr. Worm in horror. "That totally moldy Baroness!"

"A body-nabber!" cried Hetty Hyssop. "Quick, Tom, bite your tongue! You, too, Mr. Worm!"

"Thiiiiis iiiiis my castle!" hissed Mrs. Worm in the spookiest voice Tom had ever heard. "Go awaaaaay!"

"The salt water, Tom!" cried Hetty. "Squirt some on her feet!"

Tom held the spray bottle right up and squirted all the remaining salt water onto Mrs. Worm's feet.

"Eeeeeeeurgh!" wailed the Baroness. Mrs. Worm hopped up and down like crazy as a greenish gray muddy puddle grew all around her.

"Iiiii'll beeee baaaack!" howled the vile voice. Mrs. Worm's face turned blurry again, her head stopped glowing, her hair turned back to gray – and the ghost was gone.

"My darling!" Worried, Mr. Worm rushed over to his wife.

"She was – *hic* – inside – *hic* – me!" sobbed Mrs. Worm. "Oh, it was so – *hic* – dreadful, absolutely dreadful."

Her husband took her in his arms to comfort her.

"And now – *hic* – I've – *hic* – got hiccups as well!" cried Mrs. Worm despairingly.

"Don't worry!" said Hetty Hyssop. "It'll pass after about twenty-four hours. That's a typical consequence of a body-nabber attack."

"Twenty – *hic* – four – *hic* – hours!" cried Mrs. Worm, and was overcome by such a violent attack of hiccups that she couldn't utter another word.

"Hugo!" cried Tom. "Hugo, for goodness' sake, where have you been?"

"Here!" Grinning, Hugo wobbled out of a suit of armor. "Hey, that was quiiiiite sooooomething, eh? A reeeeal ghoooostly artist. Impresssssssive. Reeeeally impresssssssive, don't you agreeeeee?"

"Well, I think I can resist the attraction!" said Tom. "Can you still smell something?"

Hugo sniffed, and shook his head. "Gone!" he said disconsolately. "Miiiiiiles away!"

Hetty Hyssop nodded. "Yes, it's still light, and most ghosts can't manage much haunting when it's light. Let's make the most of it! I hope it's not much farther to the armory."

Mr. Worm shook his head.

"OK, then let's go."

The Worms, their legs trembling, obeyed, and led the ghosthunters farther through the dark castle.

"My dear Tom," whispered Hetty as they followed the couple, "that's one powerful opponent. Powerful and malicious. I fear we've got an uncomfortable night ahead of us. What do you think?"

Unfortunately, Tom could only agree.

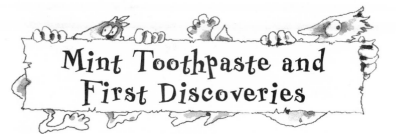

Mint Toothpaste and First Discoveries

"Here — *hic* — it is," said Mrs. Worm, opening a high, narrow door in one of the towers. A delicious warmth flooded out toward them from the former castle armory.

The large, round room was stuffed full of dented armor, smashed-up lances, broken china, and soot-encrusted paintings. The tools Mr. Worm used to fix all this were piled up on a big table. Next to it was a sofa covered in something rather moth-eaten, with a small table standing in front of it carrying two cups and a teapot. A kettle stood on a trunk in the corner and a fire was burning in the grate. Hetty Hyssop nodded in satisfaction. "Very cozy," she declared. "Tom, please make sure the doors and windows are secured. This kind of ghost usually doesn't come through the walls, but I am not sure about closed doors."

Tom went to work immediately. He fished a tube of mint toothpaste out of his backpack and started to paint

the door frames with it while Hugo wobbled over to one of the big windows and settled himself in front of the cool windowpane. The warm air from the fire took so much out of him that his feet were already turning red.

"Just look at this!" moaned Mr. Worm. He tugged at his head and held up a handful of hair. "This haunting is making it fall out in clumps! I'm definitely in urgent need of a cigar."

"I wouldn't if I were you!" Hetty Hyssop said while she hung up her coat in front of the fireplace and put the bags containing all her equipment on the table.

"Ghosts are crazy for nicotine. You don't want that moldy Baroness to pay you another visit, do you?"

Mr. Worm quickly put his cigar back in its box. Tom, meanwhile, had painted the window frames with mint paste as well.

"Well, I've put salt all over the windowsills and mint toothpaste on the door and window frames," he said. "And I've put a few handfuls of salt by the door, too. Anything else?"

"Put the **GIHUFO** seismograph on the table," Hetty Hyssop replied. "I don't want to be caught unawares again."

Tom nodded and pulled from his backpack a small device that looked like a radio. "GIHUFO is the abbreviation for **G**host **I**n **HU**man **FO**rm," explained Tom. "This thing tells us immediately if a ghost of this species is anywhere around!"

"I see," murmured the Worms, looking at the ghosthunters in fascination.

"If our precautions should turn out to be to no avail," said Hetty Hyssop, "then please remember one thing at all cost: Bite your tongue as soon as a ghost comes anywhere near. And" — she reached into one of her pockets —

"suck on these lozenges. They taste vile, but they're very reliable protection against body-nabbers."

The Worms obediently put the lozenges in their mouths. Tom and Hetty also took one each.

"Me, too?" asked Hugo.

"Nonsense," said Tom. "No ghost can slip into another. You know that full well."

"Mr. Worm," said Hetty Hyssop, "you recognized the ghost, didn't you?"

"Oh yes!" cried Mr. Worm. "Today was the first time she's shown herself so clearly. But I recognized her immediately. Immediately!" He ran over to a row of portraits that were leaning against the wall. With trembling fingers, he turned them around one after the other. "There!" he finally cried. "There, that's her!" He lifted up the picture. A woman with piercing eyes stared out at them from a heavy gilt frame. She was wearing a flowing bloodred dress with a pale-colored collar. A dead hare hung around her shoulder.

Mr. Worm lowered his voice. "That's her, the Baroness!" he whispered. "Can you see? Down there on the frame, it says: *1623. Jaspara von Gloomstone.* I don't know much about her except her name, but she still has quite a terrible reputation in these parts, even though she has been dead for hundreds of years."

"A pity!" Hetty Hyssop sighed. "A great pity. We absolutely must find out more about her. Above all, we have to find out when and how she died — it's almost impossible to drive out **HIGA**s without this information."

"HIGAs are **HI**storical **G**hostly **A**pparitions," Tom explained to the baffled-looking Worms.

Hetty Hyssop nodded. "Yes, and they come in very different degrees of dangerousness. I fear that, in this case, we're dealing with one of the more dangerous specimens."

"I'm afraid so, too," growled Tom. "The haunting presumably gets worse when it grows dark, doesn't it?"

"Oh yes!" cried Mrs. Worm. "We barely get — *hic* — a wink of sleep, what with all — *hic* — the screeching and moaning."

"But today's the first time you've seen her?" asked Hetty Hyssop.

The Worms nodded.

"Then we've probably come at just the right moment," said Tom. "Most HIGAs get stronger and stronger when their death-day approaches. They show themselves more often and become more dangerous by the day."

"Oh, is that right?" Mr. Worm's nose was turning paler and paler.

"Have you noticed that the lights flicker when it's dark?" asked Hetty Hyssop.

"Or that the boiler goes out?" added Tom.

"Absolutely." Mrs. Worm nodded vigorously. "Yesterday – *hic* – and the evening before."

"Uh-oh," said Tom. He and Hetty exchanged worried looks.

"Sheeeee's eeeeeating the pooooower supply," breathed Hugo from the windowsill. "Is sheeeeeee a real gourmet or what?"

Hetty Hyssop cast a look outside. "It'll soon be dark. Which of you two knows where the fuse box is?"

"I do," said Mr. Worm. "Why?"

"We've got to turn off her power supply," said Tom. "Or else she'll eat up so much power that nothing and nobody will be able to chase her away."

"Precisely." Hetty Hyssop pulled a mile-long extension cord out of her bag. At one end it had a plug, and at the other it had a long metal spike. "And after we shut down the power, we'll have to go to the castle library. There is a library here, isn't there?"

Mr. Worm nodded. "It's one of her favorite haunts."

"It would be," said Tom. "The Baroness wants to stop people from finding out anything about her." He looked inquiringly at Hetty Hyssop. "What else should I take with me?"

"Apart from your backpack? Hmm. We still don't know enough about our opponent, unfortunately." Hetty Hyssop rubbed her pointy nose thoughtfully. "Right. First of all" – she indicated the long cable – "we take the **HID** – **H**eat-**I**ntensifying **D**evice. Then we definitely need the mint toothpaste, salt, lozenges to suck, the portable GIHUFO seismograph – we'll leave the other one here – and, let's see, yes, a walkie-talkie. Hugo." She turned to the ASG. "You stay here with Mrs. Worm. The poor woman has suffered enough for one day. If you get paid a visit, let me know via the other walkie-talkie. But perhaps you could also just try tickling your colleague with your icy fingers, or playing one of your other little slimy jokes on her?"

"Noooo point," said Hugo. "These jokes only work on huuuuuumans."

"Pity," said Hetty Hyssop, then raised a warning finger.

The GIHUFO seismograph began to whir and flash, first yellow, then red, then moldy green.

"Bite your tongues!" hissed Hetty Hyssop. "And suck! Suck!"

A faint murmuring could be heard outside the door, followed by a scraping, as if fingernails were scratching the old wood.

"Yoooou looooowdooooown piiiiieces ooooof diiiirt!" breathed a hideously muffled voice. "Miiiiserable – aaaaahhhhh!" It broke off with a shrill scream, and a terrible clattering started up outside, as if giant feet were dancing on the old oak floorboards. Then an icy breath floated under the door, and the ghost screeched shrilly once more – and all went quiet.

Tom grinned, satisfied. "Securing the door works. Yes, yes, salt is a painful thing for ghosts' feet. Hugo, just make sure you put on your shoes, because I'm going to sprinkle salt around the whole castle, OK?"

"OK," breathed Hugo, and glanced anxiously at his pale feet.

"Good." Hetty Hyssop hung the Heat-Intensifying Device over her shoulder. "Let's get down to work."

Tom picked up the saltwater spray and the portable seismograph, and Mr. Worm kissed his wife good-bye.

"Take some coffee with you, darling," said Mrs. Worm, pressing a thermos into his hands. "Strong coffee always comes in handy."

Tom wasn't quite so sure about that one, but he didn't say anything. Instead he opened the door carefully, and when the GIHUFO seismograph didn't utter a peep, the trio stepped over the muddly puddle the ghost had left behind, and got going.

A Whole Net of Ghosts

"First things first: the fuse box," said Hetty Hyssop. "Oh, it's best to use the old secret passageway for that," said Mr. Worm. "Otherwise we'd have to go outside specially."

He led the two ghosthunters through several long corridors until they reached a room with wooden paneling decorated with skillful carvings of hunting dogs.

"Now, where was it?" murmured Mr. Worm. "Oh yes."

Quickly he made his way along the left-hand wall. Somewhere around the middle he stopped and let his fingers wander over the carved jaws and snapping teeth.

"Which one looks most gruesome?" he asked Tom.

Without hesitating, Tom pointed to a huge dog with a terrifying snarl.

Mr. Worm put his hand between the needle-sharp teeth. With a soft *click*, part of the paneling swung inward to their right. One after the other, Mr. Worm,

Tom, and Hetty Hyssop bent down and slipped through the secret door. An old lantern hung right behind it. Mr. Worm lit the flame and led the two ghosthunters down a musty-smelling staircase into the depths below. Tom started counting the steps, but at some point he gave up. Finally Mr. Worm pushed the lid of a huge wine barrel to one side, and the three of them entered the castle's cellar.

"Well hidden," murmured Tom, and looked around curiously. Massive cross vaults held up the castle walls. Between them were piled crates, planks, and heaps of old stone. A couple of rats darted into the darkness. Gigantic cobwebs hung from the ceiling like dusty gray curtains.

"Wow, Hugo would love it here," said Tom, and looked at the still-silent GIHUFO seismograph. "Seems, though, that our Baroness doesn't like damp cellars."

"Oh, I think there's another reason for that," said Hetty Hyssop. "Haven't you spotted the little bite marks all over the place? And the bluish slimy trails everywhere? This place is riddled with **TIBIG**s."

"Ti – um, what?" asked Mr. Worm anxiously.

"**TI**ny **BI**ting **G**hosts," explained Tom. "Harmless things, not in the slightest bit dangerous to humans. But their big fellow ghosts have quite a lot of respect for them. TIBIGs nibble holes in other ghosts' wobbly remains, you see. Sometimes they even chomp off whole chunks of important body parts. That gets the big ones into a real state, and they have to use up an enormous amount of ghostly energy to piece themselves back together. That's probably why the Baroness doesn't dare to come down here."

"So what do these . . . these TIBIGs look like?" asked Mr. Worm. He looked around apprehensively.

"Oh, they're about as big as an orange," said Tom. "And more or less the same shape, too, but the little beasts are as green as grasshoppers and have long, pointy tongues."

"Aha," murmured Mr. Worm – and froze when two small packs of bright green TIBIGs floated by, ignoring the three humans completely.

"Perhaps we should take some of them with us," suggested Tom. "To annoy the Baroness a bit."

"Not a bad idea," said Hetty. "You sort that out, and we'll go to the fuse box."

"The fuse box, yes, of course!" Mr. Worm stammered, looking at another pack of TIBIGs floating by. "It's over there." Soon he and Hetty Hyssop had disappeared between the huge pillars and Tom was alone in the darkness.

"Now, then, let's catch some ghosts, but quite tiny ones this time," he murmured, pulling a bag from his backpack. The sticky paper strips Tom took out stank revoltingly of mouse droppings, the Tiny Biting Ghosts' favorite smell.

"Come on, you ghost-munching little beasts,"

whispered Tom, laying the paper strips on the floor. "Come on, we haven't got much time."

Then he pulled a net out of his pants pocket and hid behind a heap of large stones. He didn't have to wait long. First a rat appeared and sniffed interestedly at his shoulders, but then there came the faint growling noise that is so typical of TIBIGs sensing their favorite smell.

Flickering, they floated closer. There were eight of them. Their little eyes glowed in the darkness as they approached the little bits of paper, growling and pushing. The biggest one snapped at the others with tiny sharp teeth – and was the first to get stuck. Two others met the same fate. Screeching, they tried to free themselves whilst their fellow TIBIGs escaped, their howls echoing through the huge cellar.

Quick as a flash, Tom sprang out, threw the ghost-proof net over his three captives, and stuffed them into his backpack. Angrily they sank their little teeth into his hand, but all he felt was a faint tickling. (Luckily the TIBIGs' ghostly teeth are completely harmless to humans – a great blessing for every ghosthunter.)

"Have you got some?" asked Hetty when Tom caught up with her and Mr. Worm.

"Of course," Tom said with a grin. "Have you found the fuse box?"

Hetty Hyssop nodded. "Our ghostly Baroness is on a diet now."

Tom sighed, relieved. "Hugo," he whispered into the walkie-talkie. "Everything OK on your end?"

"All fiiiiiine," breathed Hugo.

"Good," said Tom. "Then we'll head for the library."

When Mr. Worm opened the door to the castle library, an icy-cold wind blew out at them. The large windows were wide open, and Tom heard the rain pelting down into the castle moat outside.

Hastily the two ghosthunters shut the windows while Mr. Worm stood in the doorway, holding up his lantern in horror. "Oh no!" he cried. "All the wonderful, wonderful books!"

There was barely a single book left on the high wooden shelves. They lay in a chaotic heap on the carpet, piled high on top of one another. The precious volumes were open and torn, their old pages creased beyond repair and their leather bindings smeared with slime.

"Hmm, someone's beaten us to it." Hetty Hyssop sighed. "This is surely the work of our dear Baroness."

Tom cast a worried look through the window. Dusk was already shrouding the big trees.

"Yes, it will soon be dark," said Hetty Hyssop, reading his thoughts. "But we have to risk it. Let's look for books that deal with the castle's history. The seventeenth century is what we're particularly interested in."

"We'd better start with the ones at the bottom, then," suggested Tom. "If the Baroness wanted to hide particular books, they're bound to be there."

"I just hope they're not outside," said Hetty, casting a worried look out the window where, far below, the water in the moat made a slapping noise as it splashed against the walls.

The Totally Moldy Baroness

In the pale glow of Mr. Worm's lantern and Tom's flashlight, the trio pulled book after book from the chaotic pile. Tom had carefully painted the door frames with mint toothpaste and had scattered whole mountains of salt on the floor. Outside, the night became darker and darker, and the Baroness's power grew and grew. With flying fingers, Tom, Hetty Hyssop, and Mr. Worm leafed through thousands of crackly old books. They read, drank Mrs. Worm's strong coffee, and read some more: about feasts and famines, peasant uprisings, hills crowned with gallows, grisly civil wars, royal visits, great fires that destroyed half the castle, and cholera and plague that even the thick castle walls couldn't keep out.

"Sounds horrendous!" moaned Tom at some point. "I mean, I imagined it to be much more romantic."

"What?" asked Hetty Hyssop.

"Well, life in a castle!"

"No, goodness knows there was nothing remotely romantic about it," murmured Hetty. "Especially if you were one of the peasants." She turned another page and frowned. "Just a moment!" she whispered, and carefully smoothed the crumpled pages. "I think I've found something. Yes, this is our ghost. And it is as I feared. She is no mere HIGA; she is a full-fledged **GHADAP**."

"A what?" Mr. Worm asked.

"A **GH**ost with **A DA**rk **P**ast. A quite unpleasant subspecies, but we'll explain that later. Now listen:"

On 14 November 1623, Countess Jaspara of Muckwit married Baron von Gloomstone, whom she stabbed only one year later during a violent quarrel. No one, though, was brave enough to accuse her of that ruthless murder, and the Baroness established a regime of terror after her husband's death.

Jaspara quickly gained the nickname "the Totally Moldy Baroness," because after a hunt she liked to ride across the fields covered in blood, the stains of which promptly rotted her resplendent royal robes. Indeed, hunting was her favorite hobby, and the Totally Moldy Baroness sold her peasants into war in order to keep buying new horses and dogs, while

doubly earning her epithet by personally executing poach-
ers by throwing them into the castle moat. Her victims were
innumerable. Nevertheless, she ruled for more than ten years
before she finally received her just punishment. The youngest
sister of her murdered husband . . .

Hetty Hyssop paused, raised her head, and listened.

"What is it?" asked Tom, worried.

Hetty laid a warning finger on her lips. "Can you hear that?" she whispered.

"A horse!" cried Mr. Worm. "It sounds like a horse!"

Yes, it did. Galloping hooves resounded through the long corridors of the castle. The shrill clattering came closer and closer, and the GIHUFO seismograph in Tom's hands whirred and flashed like crazy.

"Watch out!" yelled Tom. The galloping hooves reverberated in his ears. "Watch out, she's coming!"

With a piercing screech the Baroness flew through the closed library door on her ghostly horse. Snorting, the horse landed just a few feet from poor Mr. Worm. It rolled its red eyes and flared its nostrils. Its mane tossed in the air, writhing like a bundle of snakes. The Baroness sat firmly in the saddle with her hair flying. In her hand she carried a gigantic sword, which she waved wildly in the air. She looked truly hideous, and her eyes glowed red in their dark sockets. With her hair all over the place and a cuirass fastened over her flowing dress, she grinned down at the ghosthunters.

"Giiiiive me the boooook!" she cried threateningly, and her pale hand reached through the air.

Whimpering, Mr. Worm cowered on the floor. Tom, though, quickly jumped up and threw salt into the ghostly horse's nostrils.

"You're not having the book!" he cried. "Forget about it!"

Hetty Hyssop was on her feet as well. She rammed the metal spike of the Heat-Intensifying Device into the floor and grabbed the cable from her shoulder, while Tom threw more salt at the terrible horse. Then Hetty twirled the cable above her head like a lasso and, with a sure hand, threw the plug right into the Baroness's mouth. Shocked, the dreadful ghost shut her mouth, opened it again, and tried to spit out the plug. But she simply couldn't manage it.

The library became warmer and warmer and warmer. The spike began to glow red. The Baroness

and her horse wavered, their silhouettes blurring as if they were made of liquid.

"Aaaaahhhh!" shrieked the Baroness as her horse reared up beneath her on wobbly legs. "Stooooop, stooooop aaaaat ooooonceeeee!"

But Hetty Hyssop, of course, had no intention of stopping.

"Doesn't it taste very nice, Jaspara?" she cried.

The ghost screeched angrily, wrenched her horse around, spurred him on, and galloped toward one of the windows. With a huge leap, the ghostly horse and its hideous rider sprang through the glass and plunged into the moat.

Mr. Worm, Tom, and Hetty Hyssop ran to the window just in time to see the ghostly Baroness sinking down into the seething water.

Tom leaned against the wall with a sigh. "Well, there must be some pretty interesting things about that woman in the book," he said.

"Let's hope so!" Hetty Hyssop replied.

Mr. Worm was still standing at the window, staring down into the dark water.

"She'll be back!" he muttered.

"No two ways about it!" said Hetty Hyssop. "And

all too soon, I fear. Come on, Mr. Worm." She pulled him gently away from the window. "Let's go back to your wife. In the armory we can hopefully finish the book about the Baroness in peace."

"What was that thing you used to drive her away?" asked Mr. Worm, full of astonishment.

"Oh, the HID? That's something I invented myself," said Hetty Hyssop, hoisting the cable back over her shoulder. "A Heat-Intensifying Device. Takes power away from power-supply-guzzling ghosts and turns it into what they like least of all: warmth."

"Quite amazing," murmured Mr. Worm. "Really, quite astounding."

Outside the library door, the floor was covered with slippery wet mud. Tom listened very intently for the sound of clattering hooves making their way back through the dark castle. But all remained silent.

Ghost with a Dark Past

When Mrs. Worm heard all about the goings-on in the library, she started to hiccup so violently that she had to lie down on the sofa.

"Shoooooould I scaaaaare her a bit?" breathed Hugo helpfully. "Tickle her with my iiiiiicy fingers, maybeeeee? What doooo yooooou think?"

"No," said Tom. "But you can keep your eye on the doors and windows. Who knows when that moldy Baroness will come back."

"How booooooring!" breathed Hugo. "Noooooobody toooo scare, noooothing to eeeeeat except spiiiiiders!"

"Now listen to this!" cried Hetty Hyssop. She was sitting by the fire with the fat old book that Jaspara's ghost had been so keen to snatch from her. "It says here that this 'Totally Moldy' Baroness was pushed into the moat at daybreak on her thirty-fifth birthday by her sister-in-law, and that she died an awful death by drowning. Which means . . ."

"But that's — *hic*." Mrs. Worm's face turned bright red. "That's te — *hic* — terr — *hic* . . ."

"Terrible? Oh, I think she got what she deserved," said Tom. "But it means that she's not only a GHADAP but one of the worst kinds, as she was murdered." He shook his head. "Quite a diabolical combination."

"GHADAP?" Mr. Worm asked, and looked at Hetty Hyssop. "You mentioned this before?"

"**GH**ost with **A DA**rk **P**ast," explained Tom.

"GHADAP, dark past." Mrs. Worm shook her head uncomprehendingly. "What — *hic* — on earth — *hic* — does all that mean for us?"

"Well." Hetty Hyssop sank down onto the sofa with a sigh. "I think the best way to show you is for Tom to turn on his computer."

"Just doing it," said Tom, putting his small portable laptop on the table. "Ugh!" he cried. "Hugo, have you been sliming around my computer again?"

"Ooooooh," breathed Hugo. "Juuuuuust a bit. Aaaaa little biiiiiit."

"If I catch you doing it again, I'm putting salt on it," scolded Tom. "Got it?"

"Yeah, yeah," grumbled Hugo. "You're sooooooo meeeeeeean."

Tom threw the napkin that he had used to wipe off the slime at Hugo and lifted up the screen. "Thank goodness the battery's fully charged," he said. "Otherwise we would have been up the creek without any power."

Quick as lightning, Tom's fingers darted across the keyboard. RICOG appeared on the small screen. FILE A-O. SEARCH TERM: GHADAP.

"That's it," murmured Tom. "Here we go." The screen instantly filled with text, when he pressed ENTER.

"Read it out loud," said Hetty Hyssop.

And Tom read:

GHADAP: GHost with A DArk Past

The broad category of HIGAs has many subcategories. It is known for a fact that one of these is particularly difficult to fight: the GHADAP. This type of ghost is already known before death for its extraordinarily unpleasant human characteristics, and these are only enhanced in its afterlife. GHADAPs who meet a violent end are particularly nasty. These very unpleasant ghosts possess a hideous body–nabbing capacity, sliding into and taking over living beings. This unappealing process leaves the victim in a state of serious mental confusion, with the

unfortunate side effect of violent hiccups that can last up to twenty-four hours.

Mrs. Worm sighed – amidst two hiccups – and her husband pressed her hand while Tom continued reading.

Little is known about fighting GHADAPs with body-nabbing capabilities, as each one is so individual that any kind of generalizing would be dangerous when it comes to confronting them.

However, one thing is certain: We must emphasize that it is only possible to drive GHADAPs out at the hour of their own death. If that information cannot be ascertained, any attempt to get rid of one of these evil ghosts is completely pointless.

"The hour of death!" cried Mr. Worm. "Well, that's a stroke of luck. We know when that was. Dawn."

"Yeah, but when?" Tom pushed his glasses straight. "In winter or in summer? I mean, that can make a difference of hours. If we don't know the exact day, it's as good as no use at all."

The Worms looked at each other in dismay.

"Well, we can worry about that later," said Hetty Hyssop. "We'll find out one way or another. For the moment I'd love to know something about the consequences of the Baroness's damp afterlife. Type in 'GHADAP' and 'death by drowning,' would you?"

"No prob," said Tom.

The screen filled up again. And Tom read aloud once more:

GHADAP / MUWAG: MUddy WAters Ghost
If a ghosthunter comes to a haunted place and discovers mysterious mud trails, this may very well mean that he is

dealing with a MUWAG — a GHADAP who met a violent end in the water. The MUWAG is the most dangerous subspecies of the GHADAPs, as it not only — like all forms of HIGAs — sucks electric power but can draw it from all kinds of sources: plugs, cables, electrical devices, even batteries! Thanks to its energy-packed diet, a MUWAG can become so powerful that it is able to turn its opponents to liquid merely by touching them, and — this is particularly horrific — it usually takes great delight from slurping up the puddle left by its victims. By doing so it becomes even stronger.

"But that's vile!" cried Mr. Worm. "Simply vile! Thank goodness we've switched off this monster's power supply."

"Hang on a mo'," said Tom. "Just a minute." He frowned. "My computer battery is ghost-proofed, and so's our car battery. But I hope you haven't got any battery supplies anywhere?"

The Worms turned deathly pale.

"Y – y – y – y – yes we have!" stammered Mr. Worm. "In what used to be the stables, there are the Baron's cars, all with brand-new batteries. I checked them

49

only last week. The Baron collects vintage cars, you see, and he insists that they're always ready to drive."

Hetty Hyssop and Tom exchanged alarmed looks.

"Car batteries!" Tom groaned. "How many?"

"Five," replied Mr. Worm.

"Five!" Hetty Hyssop shook her head in consternation. "Oh my goodness. Where are these stables?"

"In the west – *hic* – wing of the castle," said Mrs. Worm."Where the – *hic* – horses used to be. The drawbridge – *hic* – had to be strengthened for the cars." She looked at the ghosthunters in horror. "Oh dear, you don't think . . ."

"Yes, I most certainly do!" Hetty Hyssop sprang from the sofa. "If we don't all want to *end* up as puddles to be *slurped* up by the Baroness, we've got to check out the cars as quickly as possible!"

"We're coming, too," said Mr. Worm. "Aren't we, my darling?"

Mrs. Worm readjusted her hair ribbon. "Abso – *hic* – lutely."

"I'm not sure that's such a good idea," Tom objected. "What if the Baroness has also remembered about the cars and is waiting for us outside, completely stuffed full of current?"

"And what if – *hic* – she's here in the castle," asked Mrs. Worm, her voice trembling, "and appears as soon as you're – *hic* – outside?"

"Hugo can stay behind again to protect you," suggested Tom.

The Worms gave Hugo a suspicious look – though he didn't remotely notice because he was busy snuffling around in Tom's backpack.

"Oh please, we – *hic* – really would love to come with you!" cried Mrs. Worm. "I don't – *hic* – want to be body-nabbed again."

"All right." Hetty Hyssop shrugged her shoulders. "If that's what you want. But in that case I must ask you to wear rubber boots and rubber gloves. They might help protect you somewhat if the Baroness touches you. And there's one more thing: If we encounter the Baroness and she's already sucked up the batteries . . ."

The Worms looked at her, their eyes wide with fear.

" . . . then run," said Tom. "Run as fast as you can, and run in zigzags. . . ."

"Like a haaaaaare," breathed Hugo, disappearing up to his hips in Tom's backpack.

"Yes, dart sideways like a hare." Hetty Hyssop nodded. "That usually confuses ghosts – though this one *was* a skilled huntress. But usually, if you keep changing direction, they start trembling like . . ."

" . . . like a bowl of jelly," said Tom, grinning. "In which case we could try to draw the current off her again."

He looked inquiringly at Hetty.

"What do you think about taking the ghost whistle with us, just to be on the safe side?"

Hetty Hyssop nodded again. "It won't do any harm. So, let's go. Every minute is precious."

"And what about you, Hugo?" Tom closed his

computer. "Do you want to hold down the fort here, or do you want to come with us? Hugo?"

There was no answer from the ASG.

"Oh curses, where's he got to now?" Tom looked around, annoyed.

"I think he's disappeared inside your backpack," said Mr. Worm.

"In my backpack? Oh." Tom grinned. "Well, he's bound to be straight out again."

The next moment, Hugo shot out of the backpack like a moldy green rocket.

"Aaaaaarrrrrgggghhh!" he screeched. "Tiiiiiiny Biiiiiting Ghosts! Viiiile, stiiiinkiing, meeeeean TIBIGs! They biiit my finger!"

"I'd nearly forgotten about them," said Tom, laughing. "I'll take them with me, in any case. They might still come in handy. If the Baroness screeches half as loudly as you, I'll be pretty happy."

"Very fuuuuunny," breathed Hugo, offended, sucking at his fingers. "Absoluuuutely hilariiiiouuuus!"

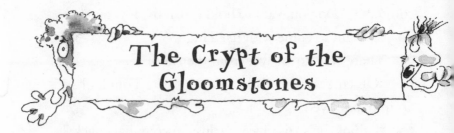

The Crypt of the Gloomstones

Hugo came with them. And so it was all five of the party that ventured out into the castle courtyard.

The day had turned to pitch-black night. The heavy rain had turned to snow, and the flakes fell damp and cold from the dark sky, covering everything.

"Ooooooooooooooooohhh!" howled Hugo. "How woooonderful. Snoooooow! It's like beeeeing in a cellar. Woooooonderful!"

"That's all we need!" groaned Tom. "Real ghost weather! The moldy Baroness will be chuffed to bits, won't she?"

Hetty Hyssop nodded. "Yes, the snow definitely works for her, but on the other hand it will be very easy in all this whiteness to see any trace of mud she leaves behind."

Mr. Worm led the way with his lantern. Mrs. Worm trotted beside him, then came Tom and Hetty

Hyssop, salt water and GIHUFO seismograph at the ready. Hugo sometimes wobbled ahead of, sometimes behind the little group. With relish, he let the snow fall gently into his mouth.

"The stables are in the west wing!" whispered Mr. Worm. "Just by the castle's outside wall."

"So what's that on the other side?" Tom pointed to the east wing of the castle.

"That's the chapel," said Mrs. Worm. "The chapel – *hic* – of the Gloomstones, with the family crypt."

"The family crypt?" asked Hetty Hyssop. "There's a family crypt here? That's very interesting!"

"The date of Jaspara's death!" cried Tom.

Mr. Worm slapped himself on the forehead. "Of course! Why didn't I think of it earlier? What an idiot!" He almost tripped over his feet with agitation.

"Chapel, crypt," murmured Hugo. "Viiiile places, quiiiite viiiile places."

"Yeah, yeah, I know," said Tom. "Graveyards, crypts, chapels . . . most ghosts don't like those sorts of places, though everybody believes they do. We most probably won't bump into the Baroness there!"

When they finally reached the old stables, which were now the Baron's garage, both Tom and Hetty

Hyssop looked around carefully, but there was nothing suspicious to be seen or heard. And the GIHUFO seismograph didn't utter a peep.

"Mr. Worm," said Hetty Hyssop, "I suggest you and your wife take care of the car batteries. But whatever you do, don't take them with you, as that would lure the Baroness in your direction. Just pour this solution on them. That'll make them inedible to ghosts for a while. Here's a walkie-talkie, as well." She passed the radio to the Worms along with two little bottles. "Hugo, you stay with the pair of them, and howl down the walkie-talkie as soon as you smell anything ghostlike. Then we'll be with you right away."

"Yeah, yeah," breathed Hugo. "Iiiii'll doooo it. Though I woooould liiiiike tooooo get tooooo know the Baroness a bit better. Her ghooosting skiiill reeeally is quiiiite fantaaaastic, and she doesn't look tooooo bad, eeeeeither, oh nooooo!"

"The woman is hideous!" said Tom. "So don't you turn all romantic on us, got it?"

"Ooooh, but Iiiii'm hideooous, toooooo!" breathed Hugo. "That woooooouldn't booooother meeeee."

Tom rolled his eyes. "Great! You sound positively in love! In love with a goggle-eyed monster!"

"Ruuubbish!" Hugo howled and gave Tom an irritated shove in the chest. "What ruuuubbish!"

Tom laughed so much that his glasses slipped down his nose. "It'll be hot stuff when you two press your icy fingers together. Know what, Hugo? You should just pay her a couple of ghostly compliments when she appears. Perhaps they'll make her forget that she wants to turn us into mud puddles and slurp us up, OK?"

"Very fuuuunny!" Hugo blew his moldy breath into Tom's face. "Absoluuuutely hilarioooous!"

"Oh, stop it, you two," said Hetty. "We really don't have time for that sort of thing. Mr. Worm, have you got the key to the chapel and the crypt?"

"Of course." Mr. Worm pulled a huge bunch of keys from his pocket. "It's that one there, the long ornate one."

Hetty Hyssop pocketed it and gave the GIHUFO seismograph to Mr. Worm. "Here," she said, "in case worse comes to worst. You're probably best off not relying on Hugo if his head's all swirling with romance. Come on, Tom."

"See you, Hugo!" Tom laughed. "And don't pine too much for your pinup girl, OK? Otherwise she'll really appear."

"Ha-haaaaaa!" breathed Hugo, throwing a snowball at Tom's head. Tom shook the snow out of his hair and answered with a snowball through Hugo's pale chest. Then he hurried after Hetty Hyssop, who was marching across the snow-covered courtyard toward the crypt of the Gloomstones. . . .

The snow was already piled so high that their boots disappeared into it up to their ankles and there was nothing to be heard but the crunch of frozen footsteps. Tom let his eyes wander across the dark windows that surrounded them, like he had done upon their arrival, but this time he didn't sense eyes staring at him.

"Thank goodness," he murmured.

"What?" asked Hetty Hyssop.

"Oh, nothing," Tom replied, wiping a couple of snowflakes from his glasses. "I guess it's that door over there, under the coat of arms."

He was right. When Hetty Hyssop turned the key in the lock, the door swung open with a groan, and they found themselves standing in the crypt of the Gloomstones. It smelled of damp stone, candle wax — and mud.

"Look at that," whispered Hetty Hyssop. "It seems like our moldy Baroness is not as afraid of crypts as Hugo is."

Dark traces of mud led along the aisle between the rows of carved choir stalls and disappeared into the darkness behind the altar.

Tom bent down. "These traces seem to be quite old," he whispered.

Cautiously, they went on. A second space opened up behind the altar, a space with several large stone slabs on the wall. Most of them were guarded by weeping angels, stony tears in their marble eyes.

Tom slowly cast his torch over the inscriptions on the slabs.

"Giselbert, Ethelgar, Miesgunde," read Tom. "Gee, they had funny names. I wonder . . ." He got no further.

A crackling came from the walkie-talkie.

"Hello, hello!" whispered Mr. Worm's agitated voice. "Please say something!"

"What's wrong?" asked Hetty Hyssop.

"She did get here first after all! The batteries have been sucked up!" cried Mr. Worm. "All of them. It looks terrible. What should we do now?"

"Come over to the crypt right away!" said Hetty Hyssop. "As quickly as you can."

"Bad news," murmured Tom. He cast his flashlight onto the next slab, which was guarded by two marble dogs. The inscription was competely covered in mud. Tom pulled out his pocketknife and carefully scratched away the filth.

"'Jaspara, Baroness von Gloomstone,'" he read. "'Treacherously murdered at dawn on the twelfth of May, sixteen fifty-eight. Born on the same day in sixteen twenty-three.'"

"May." Hetty Hyssop rubbed the tip of her nose. "When does the sun rise in May?"

"Just a sec." Tom pulled a little calendar out of his pants pocket. "Sunrise in May — here. Four-forty. So that's the only time the Baroness is vulnerable." He looked at his watch. "It's just past midnight now. That gives us a bit of time to decide what to do."

"I fear there's not much to decide." Hetty Hyssop looked thoughtfully at the old gravestone. "I know of only two methods for helping such a strong GHADAP to find eternal rest."

"I know one as well," said Tom. "You write the ghost's name backward on a mirror, and somehow get it to look at it. Then it vaporizes."

"Mmm!" Hetty nodded. "But I once tried that method years ago with a ghost who'd drowned — just like our Baroness. The mirror exploded and the ghost chased me around his castle three times. I was only saved because I somehow managed to get into my ghost-proof car. A dreadful experience. Quite apart from the fact that I had so many glass splinters sticking into me that I looked like a hedgehog."

"And the ghost?" asked Tom. "What happened to the ghost?"

"He went on to liquidize three colleagues," said Hetty Hyssop, "until the famous Italian ghosthunter Professor Boccabella destroyed him."

"What with?" asked Tom. "How did he manage that?"

"By using an incredibly dangerous method," said Hetty. "He . . ."

The radio crackled again.

"Help!" cried Mr. Worm, his voice cracking. "Heeeeeelp! She's coming. She's coooooming!"

At the Last Minute

When Tom and Hetty Hyssop ran out of the chapel, a hideous sight met their eyes. The snowy courtyard was glowing blue in the ghostly light of the moldy Baroness. Following her car-battery feast, she and her terrible horse were gigantic; so gigantic that the Baroness's gruesome, moldy head rose up above the castle wall. Screeching and howling, she tore behind the poor Worms, who were running zigzag across the snow like terrified hares. There was no sign what-soever of Hugo.

"Quick, Tom, the whistle!" cried Hetty Hyssop, pulling the HID from her shoulder. The Baroness was just stretching out a pale hand to Mrs. Worm, who managed to avoid the icy fingers only at the very last minute.

"Curses," muttered Hetty Hyssop. "I can't get the spike to stay in the ground. What on earth's going on? Hey!" she cried. "Hey, Jaspara, you monster, come over here! Or are you afraid?"

The ghastly Baroness swung her horse around and stared down at the two ghosthunters with her red eyes.

Exhausted and grateful for a breather, the Worms collapsed into the snow.

"Whaaaaat?" howled Jaspara, her snorting horse prancing closer. "Whaaaaat diiiiid sheeeee saaaaay?"

"Since when have you had a hearing problem?" Tom fearlessly took a couple of steps toward the giant ghostly horse. "She called you a monster. And that's exactly what you are — or haven't you had a chance to look in a mirror for the last few hundred years?" *Talk, Tom, talk*, he ordered himself, while his fingers were desperately searching his pockets for the whistle.

Jaspara bent over her horse's neck with a murderous smile. "I'll kill youuuuuu!" she moaned with her horrible voice. "Iiiiiii will kiiiiiill you right noooooow."

"Oh yes? I don't think so!" Tom cried. His fingers had finally found the whistle and he blew into it with all his might.

Nothing could be heard — by human ears, at any rate. Jaspara's ghostly horse, however, reared up so wildly that the Baroness lost her grip and fell backward into the snow. Tom blew again and the horse galloped

away toward the castle gate, casting its bluish light onto the snow.

"Now!" cried Tom.

Hetty Hyssop drove the spike into the snow with all her might and threw the HID plug at Jaspara once again. This time, though, it didn't land in her mouth but wrapped itself, together with its cable, around her throat. The metal spike flew after it and lay on her chest like a piece of strange jewelry.

Slowly, very slowly, the spike began to glow.

"Aaaaargh!" shrieked Jaspara, tearing through the cable with one jerk and hurling both pieces into the snow. Reeling, she got back to her feet.

"She's already too powerful!" cried Hetty Hyssop. "Let's hope the HID had a chance to work."

The Worms were still crouching in the snow. Horrified, they looked up at the Baroness as she came floating toward them with a horrible grin.

"Look!" Tom shouted. "It *has* worked! She's shrinking! She's shriveling up again!"

And it was true: The Baroness was becoming smaller. Steaming, her pale limbs started to shrivel, whilst the snow all around her turned into a bluish shimmering slush.

"Aaaaargh!" she screeched angrily, raising herself into the air and floating toward the poor Worms yet again.

"The Tiny Biting Ghosts!" cried Hetty Hyssop. "Quick, Tom, let them out!"

The TIBIGs. Of course! Tom cursed himself for not having remembered them earlier. With trembling hands he wrenched off his backpack. The Worms were running zigzag across the courtyard again, but their legs could barely carry them, and the Baroness was gaining on them, laughing mockingly.

"Come on out, you lot!" cried Tom, shaking the backpack. "Out, you little beasts!"

The net full of TIBIGs dropped into the snow. Tom tore the net apart, and the little ghosts made off in all directions, growling and snapping.

The Baroness looked around in horror.

"Aaaaargh!" she screeched. "Cursed ghost-eaters!" Angrily she tried to shake off the little beasts, but they had already bitten their way through her flowing ghostly robes. They almost sounded like a pack of tiny dogs as they snapped at her pale limbs, yelping and gnashing their jaws triumphantly. The Baroness flailed at them with her riding crop, but that made the TIBIGs even angrier. They bit whole chunks out of the bigger ghost until the already moldy Baroness looked like a slice of Swiss cheese. Mrs. Worm watched with delighted horror, till her husband grasped her hand and made her run with him toward the two ghosthunters. "Will the little — *hic* — things eat her up?" asked Mrs. Worm hopefully while she hid behind Hetty Hyssop.

"Unfortunately not," Hetty Hyssop replied. "But they'll divert her attention away from us for a while. So let's get a move on. With a bit of luck, she won't get rid of the little ghosts until we're safely back in the armory."

Their legs were as heavy as lead when they started running again. Snow swirled into their eyes, the castle's main door seemed miles away, and they could still hear the Baroness's furious screeching behind them. When Tom took a quick look back, her head was just dropping into the snow, but she angrily replaced it, kicked a TIBIG over the castle wall like a soccer ball, and unceremoniously swallowed another.

"Where in the world is Hugo?" cried Hetty when they finally stumbled up the castle steps.

"She blew him over the castle wall!" Mr. Worm gasped and opened the heavy door. "We didn't see him again after that."

"She's coming – *hic* – behind us again!" cried his wife. And sadly she was right. The Baroness came floating toward them, one TIBIG still snapping at her arms. The sight of her was even more horrible with all the holes in her moldy, ghostly shape.

"Tom, squirt salt water – quickly!" yelled Hetty Hyssop while she pushed the Worms through the door.

Tom obeyed – though it was hard to squirt the water without just hitting one of the holes the TIBIGs had torn into the Baroness. He almost stumbled over his own feet, turning and squirting over and over again while he was running with the others down the endless corridors of the castle. He felt like his lungs would burst at any moment, hearing the Baroness howl and curse behind them as she came closer and closer, until Tom hit her again with the salt water and she slowed down once more. Half dead with exhaustion, the ghosthunters finally reached the door to the armory.

Using the last of their strength, they slipped inside. Tom quickly painted the door frames with mint toothpaste again, scattered the last bit of salt in front of the door, and then collapsed, exhausted, onto the old sofa.

"What if she comes through the door?" he asked, breathing heavily. "What if she's still strong enough?"

"Well," Hetty Hyssop whispered, "then all we can do is hope she's too weak to liquidize any of us. If we want to drive her out – for good – then we need time – as well as a couple of other things."

They all listened, but it was silent outside.

Very silent.

Till suddenly the GIHUFO seismograph in Mr. Worm's hand whirred and flashed like crazy.

"Split up!" cried Hetty Hyssop. "She's coming. Mr. Worm, grab some logs from the basket and set them alight in the fireplace – one for each of us. She won't like flames. And everyone, bite your tongue!"

And so they stood there, each of them in their own corner, holding the burning pieces of wood, biting their tongues, and waiting.

But not for long.

They knew the scratching and scraping at the door only too well.

"Aaargh!" yelled Mr. Worm. "Her hand! Look, her hand!"

Slowly, very slowly, the Baroness's pale, moldy hand pushed its way through the wooden door.

"The salt's not working!" whispered Tom. "Oh my goodness, it's not stopping her!"

Mrs. Worm started to sob quietly.

But then Tom heard something else. . . .

Hugo Makes His Entrance

"Haaaaa-haaaaa!" howled Hugo in the corridor outside. "Ha, Jaspara, yoooou old misery. Do yoooou know where Iiiii ended up? In the mooooooat, right in the middle of that muddy, stiiiinking mooooot."

Jaspara's hand retreated.

Mrs. Worm started to sob again, this time with relief.

"Whaaaaat dooooooooo yoooouuuuuu waaaaant, yoooouuuuu coooommooooon meeeaaaaasly spooook?" demanded the Baroness in her horrible voice.

"Oh, Hugo, take care," murmured Tom. "Just take care."

"What dooooo Iiiii want?" breathed Hugo. "Ooooh, Iiiii want to annooooy yoooou, yoooou big-mooooouthed diiiimwiiiit. I juuust want to annooooy yooooou a biiiiit."

"Fooorgeet iiit!" growled Jaspara. "Iii'vee nooot goot tiiiimeee foor suuuch siiiilliiiineeess. Iiii'd raaaatheeer liiiiquuuiiiidiiiiizeee aaaa cooooouuuupleeee ooof juuuiiicy huumaaans aaand sluuurp theeem uuup."

As silently as a shadow, Tom crept to the keyhole and peered through. He was amazed by what he saw.

Hugo was wobbling around quite close to the Baroness, who was still remarkably large. He was tugging at her robes, sticking his tongue out at her, pointing his fingers through her holes, and behaving in a generally childish way.

What was he up to?

"Loook!" piped Hugo. He waved his fingers about in the air and *whisk*! The Baroness's head was in his hand.

"Unbelievable!" whispered Tom, astonished. "Completely unbelievable!"

"What is it?" asked Mr. Worm, his voice trembling. "Wh – wha – what's going on?"

"I don't get it," said Tom. "Hugo's got her head."

"Aaaaargh!" screeched the head, its teeth snapping at Hugo's fingers – whereupon he stuck it under his arm without any further ado.

"Puuuut myyy heeeeeaaaaad baaaaack!" howled the headless Baroness. "Nooooow!"

"No!" Grinning broadly, Hugo wobbled to and fro in front of the Baroness's headless body. "Yoooou'll have tooooooo come and fetch iiiit."

"Yoooooouuuuuu loooooouuuuuusy puuuuukeee-greeeeen mooooooldy ghooooost!" howled the head, and spat on the ASG's foot.

Hugo answered this by taking Jaspara's head in both hands, bouncing it on the ground three times like a rather unsavory basketball – and throwing it through a window. It landed outside.

"Go and looooook for iiiit!" he howled contentedly. "Loooook for iiiit. But don't run iiiinto the wall, Baroness Not-So-Bright!"

The headless Baroness lunged at him, but quick as lightning Hugo wobbled past the arms that were waving angrily all over the place and slipped through the wall into the armory.

"Soooo?" he breathed down the speechless Tom's ear. "How was Iiiiii?"

"Unbelievable, Hugo," said Tom admiringly. "Total respect, my friend, you were just stunning!"

He peered through the keyhole again. The Baroness was drifting down the corridor in search of her head – which was not, of course, terribly easy, given that she had no eyes.

"She's gone," he said, turning back to the others.

"She's gone to look for her head, but that might take her a while. Hugo chucked it through the window."

"Oooh!" the Worms sighed, staring at Hugo with admiration.

"Splendid, old fellow," said Hetty Hyssop. "How did you do it?"

"It was nooooothiiing!" breathed Hugo, but he inflated himself right up to the ceiling with pride. "Before she blew me oooout of the castle coooourtyard, Iiiii wanted to pay her a cooooouple of cooooompliments and" – he turned red with embarrassment – "kiss her hand. But suddenly Iiiiii had her fiiingers iiin *my* hand. Stuck toooo them. Just like that."

"Interesting," murmured Hetty Hyssop. "Carry on."

"It made her rather angry, and she blew me over the castle wall iiiinto the moooooat. That annoyed meeee, and so Iiiii thooooought that if her fiiiingers got stuck toooo my hand" – he gave a hollow giggle – "then her head wooooould probably get stuck to it, tooooo."

"Cunning, very cunning," said Hetty Hyssop with a laugh. "And of course you knew that you could slip through the wall while she was dependent on doors and windows, didn't you?"

"Preciiiiisely!" breathed Hugo. "Sheeee's probably stiiiill looooooking for her head. It'll beeeee rather snowed iiiin." Hugo's pale body wobbled with laughter.

Tom looked inquiringly at Hetty. "Couldn't that help us get rid of her once and for all?"

"It's entirely possible," Hetty Hyssop said. "But how? Let's have a think." She turned to the Worms. "Come on, let's all sit together for a moment. It's now" – she looked at the clock – "nearly two o'clock. So we've still got a bit of time. I'd like to tell you quickly about the only successful exorcism of a GHADAP that I know of – a GHADAP who had similar abilities to our Baroness." Hetty Hyssop rubbed her pointy nose. "It was many years ago, and Professor Boccabella, who managed to get rid of it, told me about it himself. At first he proceeded as we've done: He switched off the power, got rid of all other sources of energy – which we didn't manage to do, unfortunately – and then he found out the time and place where the ghost died. . . ."

"The place?" Mr. Worm interrupted her. "Do we know the place?"

"Too right," said Tom. "She was pushed in from the drawbridge. We don't yet know exactly where."

Hetty Hyssop nodded. "But what happened next? Professor Boccabella had an extremely daring but, as it turned out, very effective idea. . . ."

"Oh, tell – *hic* – us!" cried a breathless Mrs. Worm.

There was a deathly silence in the armory. Only the wood on the fire crackled gently.

"Well," continued Hetty Hyssop, "first Boccabella used a trail of skillfully planted batteries to lure the rather hungry ghost to the place where it had died. Unfortunately we don't have this option. The Baroness is unlikely to be hungry now. But Hugo's skills might help us again here."

"Oh, sooooo Iiiiii'm goiiiiing to beeeee the bait," breathed Hugo.

"Yes, if it comes to it," said Hetty Hyssop. "So, anyway, Boccabella lured the ghost to the place where it died. And" – Hetty lowered her voice – "and he waited for him there, dressed in an old cloak that the ghost himself had worn while he was still alive."

"Oh, we've – *hic* – got one of the Baroness's – *hic* – dresses!" cried Mrs. Worm excitedly. "I think it's – *hic* – the same one she's wearing in the portrait."

"Excellent." Hetty Hyssop sighed, relieved. "Then it could work."

"Oh, please, tell us more!" Mr. Worm urged her. "Boccabella waited for the ghost. Then what happened?"

"He had a courageous plan," Hetty Hyssop continued. "He wanted to provoke the ghost into touching him."

"But" — Mrs. Worm put her hand to her mouth in horror — "wasn't he — *hic* — afraid of being liquidized and sucked up? "

"No, for Boccabella knew one thing for certain," Hetty Hyssop continued. "He knew that a GHADAP is terrified of touching anything from its human past. The more contact a GHADAP had with this object during its life, and the closer the contact was, the more anxious it is to avoid touching it now in the present. The only thing this evidently doesn't apply to is the building it lived in. Boccabella observed on several occasions how GHADAPs recoil from old bed linens, suits of armor, or items of clothing, as if the devil himself were hiding in them. So he took a gamble and tried using the old cloak to protect himself from being liquidized. At the same time he hoped that the ghost would be destroyed on the spot when it touched the cloak."

"And?" asked Tom, on tenterhooks. "Did it work?"

Hetty Hyssop nodded. "The ghost turned to mist and vanished."

"Wow," Tom murmured. "Pretty brave of this Boccabella fellow, I have to say."

"Miiist." Hugo sighed. "Miiist and vaaaanished. What a piiiity! Iiiii had soooo much fun with the Baroness."

Tom cast him an annoyed glance, but Hetty Hyssop turned to the Worms.

"So . . . where do we find this dress?"

"It's here!" Mrs. Worm explained triumphantly. "It had — *hic* — a little hole in it, and I brought it over here to — *hic* — be repaired a few days ago."

Excited, she trotted over to an old cupboard behind a couple of bashed-up suits of armor, and came back with a red dress. It was undoubtedly the same dress that the Baroness was wearing in her portrait.

"Oh dear!" said Tom. "Who's that supposed to fit, then?"

"I'm afraid you're too plump, my love," said Mr. Worm to his wife. "And Hetty Hyssop is much too tall."

"Well, people were much smaller back then," said Hetty Hyssop. "And the Baroness is much bigger as a ghost than she was when she was alive. Hmm." She

81

rubbed the tip of her nose thoughtfully. "I fear there's only one person here who'll fit into the dress."

"Who?" asked Tom.

Hugo gave him a nasty smile. "Yooooou," he breathed. "Whoooo else?"

"Me?" Tom looked at the others in astonishment. "Me? Are you joking? There's no way I'm putting on a dress."

"Of course not." Hetty Hyssop shook her head. "I couldn't agree with you more. It would be far too dangerous. After all, who can say whether Boccabella's method works on all GHADAPs? And there's no way I want to take you home in a water bottle."

"Oh no, that's not what I meant!" cried Tom. "I don't mean it's too *dangerous* for me!" He hadn't given that a moment's thought. "But I can't, I mean . . ." He turned beet red. "I'm not standing out there on the drawbridge in a dress. It's . . ." Awkwardly, he set his glasses straight. "It's embarrassing."

"Ha-ha-ha-ha-ha!" Hugo laughed, tapping Tom on the nose with an icy finger. "That's pretty stuuupid, don't yooooou thiiiiink? Ha-ha-ha-ha-ha!"

"Look who's talking," growled Tom. "You spend all your time floating around the place in that flapping thing."

"Hmm," said Hetty Hyssop. "So what do we do? We've got two hours to come up with something. That is, if our friend doesn't get back early. And she'll be pretty annoyed, that's for sure."

They all fell into a depressed silence.

Tom felt wretched. Absolutely wretched.

"Yeah, OK," he said finally. "I'll do it. I'll put the thing on. But I don't have to wear a wig or anything, do I?"

"A veil wooooooouldn't be baaaaad," breathed Hugo. "It'd suuuit yoooou down to the groooooound."

"Hugo, leave him alone," said Hetty Hyssop, standing up. "Thank you very much, Tom. You are once again a pleasure to work with. Let's get everything ready. Mrs. Worm, can you alter the dress so that the Baroness won't recognize it?"

"No – *hic* – problem," said Mrs. Worm.

"Good," said Hetty Hyssop. "Then you'd better start now. We don't have much time."

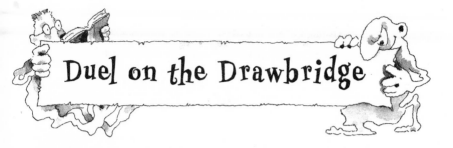

Duel on the Drawbridge

It was shortly after four a.m. when Tom stepped out onto the drawbridge with Hetty Hyssop. The night hung as black as pitch over the old castle; only the snow shimmered in the darkness. It had stopped snowing, but an icy wind was whirling around the walls and up to the chapel belfry. The bell's clanging sounded eerie as it echoed around, the only noise in the stillness of the night.

Tom shuddered. He felt awful. The Baroness's dress flapped around his arms and legs, and he was wretchedly cold despite having jeans and a sweater on underneath. And the veil he wore to keep the Baroness from recognizing him didn't make things better.

"Good grief," Tom muttered. "At least nobody can see me like this."

"Oh, come now!" said Hetty Hyssop. "In some countries men wear dresses all the time, don't they? Switch on your Spook Energy Visualizer, please."

"OK!" Tom fumbled in his clothes and brought out something that looked exactly like a flashlight, apart from the fact that it had a strangely shaped blue bulb. He clipped it to the red dress and slowly shone the blue light over the bridge.

"There!" he whispered. "That's where it must have happened."

Far to the right, on the edge of the bridge, the snow began to glow as the blue light fell on it. It swirled high into the air and fell lightly down into the dark water of the moat. A faint sigh cut through the night.

"Have you found anything?" cried Mr. Worm.

He and his wife were sitting together in a rowboat under the bridge. The pair of them had insisted on being there right to the bitter end.

"Yes, we've found the spot!" answered Hetty Hyssop. "But not another peep out of you, understood? Otherwise it's possible that the Baroness will have a go at you rather than at our well-dressed friend here."

Tom swallowed. He suddenly had a picture of long, pale fingers grasping for him. He shook his head firmly.

"Something wrong?" asked Hetty, concerned.

"No, no," said Tom. *Ghosthunters' rule*, he reminded

himself silently: *Never imagine too clearly what could happen to you. Never ever.*

Without further hesitation he gathered up the long dress and placed himself right on the spot where the snow had just swirled up. That part of the drawbridge was still glowing, but when Tom unclipped the Spook Energy Visualizer, the blue light disappeared as if someone had wiped it away.

What a strange feeling, thought Tom. *Standing exactly where Death snatched the Baroness*. For a brief moment his feet felt quite hot.

Hetty looked at the clock. "Four-thirty. It's nearly time. Are you ready, Tom? Your teeth are chattering."

"It's just the cold," Tom growled.

"Fine, then I'll give Hugo the signal!" Hetty Hyssop waved up at the belfry with a white handkerchief. Hugo was waiting there to join in.

"Listen, my dear young chap." Hetty put her arm around Tom's shoulders. "Promise me you won't play the hero. If anything seems strange to you, then run. Or jump into the moat. Promise?"

Tom nodded and looked down into the black water. A layer of ice was already forming at the edges of the moat.

"Things'd have to be pretty bad for me to jump in there," he said. "With this dress on, I'd sink like lead. No wonder the Baroness drowned, wearing all these heavy layers!"

"Well, the Worms could fish you out if need be," said Hetty Hyssop. "But I hope such measures won't be necessary. By the way, Boccabella told me that the place where the ghost touched him immediately started to itch as if he'd been stung by a nettle. If you feel anything else, then run – got it? I'll be waiting in the car at the end of the bridge. So you've only got to cover a short distance, OK?"

"OK," said Tom and tried his best to sound completely fearless.

"Good!" Hetty Hyssop clapped her hand on his shoulder again. "I really wish I were standing here instead of you, but my cursed height . . ."

"Aaaahhhhiiii!" A wailing voice came from the castle courtyard. "Ha-haaaa! It's my castle now. Yes, it's miiiiine nooooow, old girl. Oooooh, dooooon't loooook sooooo angry. Coooooome on, coooome and fetch it, coooome and fetch yoooour head, Baroness Jaspaaaaara!"

"Seems like our plan is working!" whispered Hetty Hyssop. "Hugo's lured her outside. Good luck, Tom!"

Then she quickly ran to her car, leaving Tom behind, all alone on the bridge.

The wind buffeted the red dress and tore at the long veil. Tom heard Hugo approaching; he drew closer and closer. And Tom knew who was following

89

the ASG, furious and powerful after her long night: the Baroness.

"Tra-la-la!" piped Hugo, hastily wobbling out of the dark portal. "Coooome and fetch iiiit, Baroness!"

Once again, he had the GHADAP's head clasped under his pale arm. With a nasty grin, Hugo floated up to the battlements of the castle wall and waved down at Tom. His garish green eyes glowed like those of an owl in the darkness.

They didn't have to wait long for Hugo's pursuer.

With a ghastly screech, the headless Baroness came floating onto the drawbridge. In her rage, she was flickering so brightly that the water in the moat turned shimmering silver. Jaspara's moldy arms groped searchingly through the cold air. Silently Hugo floated down to her and put her head back on her neck. The wrong way around. Then he speedily floated back onto the castle wall.

"Aaaaargh!" howled the Baroness. "Oooooh, veeeery fuuuuunny, yooooooou sliiiiimy smaaaaart aaaaaleeeeeck!" Angrily, she took off her head and put it back the right way around. "Juuuuust gooooo aaaaawaaaay! Theeeeereeee's nooooot rooooooooom foooooor twooooo ghooooosts heeeereeeee. . . ."

At that moment she spotted Tom.

She stopped in her tracks as if turned to stone. Her eyes almost popped out of their dark sockets. It was a truly terrifying sight.

"Yooooouuuuu!" the Baroness breathed threateningly. "Whooooo aaaaareeeee yooooouuuuu?"

Tom's teeth chattered like an old typewriter. Annoyed, he clamped them together.

Slowly, the Baroness floated over to Tom. She was still gigantic. Tom barely reached up to her belly button.

"Whaaaaat dooooo yooooouuuuu waaaaant heeeeereeeee?" she hissed. "Thiiiiis iiiiis my teeeeerriiiiitooooory, gooooot iiiit?"

Tom took a deep breath. Their plan was working so far. The Baroness had no idea who was standing in front of her. And she was angry. That made her blind.

"Heeeellooo, Jaspara!" trilled Tom in a high voice. "Yoouuu loooook hiiideeeooouuus. Hiiideeeooouuus aaaaas aaalwaaays."

Wow, was it ever difficult to talk like a ghost.

"Whaaaaat?" screeched Jaspara. "Whaaaaat diiiiid yooooouuuuu saaaaay, frooooog-faaaaaceeeee?"

By now the Baroness was standing so close to Tom that he could have touched her. Her revolting moldy

91

stench almost took his breath away. But if he so much as moved one step away from the spot where she had met her doom, all would be lost.

So Tom mustered up all his courage and had another go at her. "Yooouuu viiiiiile beeeeeast!" he cried in a high falsetto. "Yooouuu ooold mooooonster! You –"

The Baroness silenced him abruptly by tearing the veil from his head with one pull.

"Aaaaah!" She recoiled in surprise. "Whaaaaat's goooooiiiiing oooon? Whaaaaat's aaaaall thiiiiis aaaaabooooouuuuut? Whaaaaat gaaaaameeeee aaaaareeeee yoooooouuu plaaaaayiiiing wiiiiith meeeee, liiiiittleeeee squuuuuiiiiirt? Wiiiiith meeeee, Jaaaaaspaaaaaraaaaa voooon Glooooooooooomstooooooone?"

What was Tom supposed to say? That he wanted to destroy her and turn her into swirling fog?

It's all over! he thought. *And I'm stuck in this wretched dress! Oh well, so who cares if she turns me into a puddle.*

"Run, Tom!" shouted Hetty through the open car window. "Quickly!"

But Tom had no intention of running. After all, Boccabella hadn't run away, either.

"Get lost!" he shouted, his voice shaking just a little

bit. "You bore me to death!" He had to throw his head right back in order to look into the Baroness's evil red eyes. "You were a monster when you were human, but you're the absolute pits as a ghost!"

"Sooo?" howled Jaspara, bending down over him.

Tom froze. He turned so cold that he could barely feel a thing. Not the wind, not his fear — and he'd already lost all feeling in his feet.

Hetty Hyssop sprang out of the car and ran across to them. But just before she reached the bridge, she slipped on an iced-over puddle and plunged headlong into the moat.

"Over here!" Tom heard Mr. Worm calling. "Over here, Mrs. Hyssop!"

The Baroness paid not the slightest attention to the commotion in the moat. She only had eyes for Tom. She bent farther and farther down over him with a smile that was so abysmally evil, Tom's teeth started to chatter uncontrollably again.

"Leeeet goooooo of hiiiiim!"

Hugo appeared so suddenly behind the Baroness that even Tom turned in surprise. Blue with rage, the ASG wobbled toward the much bigger ghost. "Leeeeave hiiiiim alooooone!"

"Whaaaaat? Dooooo yooooouuuuu liiiiikeeeee theeeee yooooouuuuungster?" breathed the Baroness maliciously. "Theeeen juuuust looooooook whaaaaat Iiiii'm gooooiiiiing tooooo dooooo tooooo hiiiiim."

Hugo tried to grab hold of her head again, but this time Jaspara was ready for him. Howling, she whirled around, took a deep breath, and blew the ASG into the nearest tree.

Oh great! thought Tom, not sure whether his knees were shaking more from the cold or from fear. *Perhaps it's time I vanished, too.* But his legs wouldn't move from the spot.

"Sooooo!" howled the Baroness, flashing her red eyes at him. Tom had felt these eyes once before, when he first arrived at the castle.

"Aaaaand noooooooow iiiiit'sssss yooooouuuuuur tuuuuurn, my laaaaad." She smiled her ghastly smile again. "Iiiii'm gooooiiiiing tooooo sluuurp yooooouuuu uuuuup!" she breathed. "Aaaaah, yooooouuuuu'll beeeee taaaaasty!"

Then she reached out her hands.

Her pale fingers closed around Tom's arms like the claws of a bird of prey. But as they did so, she touched the dress as well — the very dress that had kept her human body warm so many hundreds of years ago.

Tom immediately felt the itchy, tingling sensation, just as the famous Boccabella had described it.

"Aaaaargh!" Jaspara's shriek was so terrible and piercing that Tom had to clamp his hands to his ears.

But he could still hear the hideous hissing sound – the hissing as Jaspara disintegrated. First of all her entire body turned transparent like frosted glass. Then it fell apart like a bit of threadbare rag and was blown away by the wind.

Ready for a Vacation

"Tom!" cried Hetty Hyssop from under the bridge. "Tom, where are you?"

"Everything's fine!" cried Tom, though his voice might have suggested otherwise.

"Bravooooo!" cried Hugo from up in the tree. "He vaaaporiiized her, tooootally vaaaporiiized her."

His knees trembling, Tom went over to the drawbridge railing and looked down.

"Oh, I'm so glad to see you, young man!" cried Mr. Worm, holding up his lantern. Next to him sat his wife and the sopping-wet Hetty Hyssop.

"There was such a dreadful – *hic* – noise up there!" cried Mrs. Worm. "We were – *hic* – terribly worried."

"She's gone," said Tom. "Dissolved, blown away, kaput. Professor Boccabella's method worked brilliantly!"

"My dear Tom," said Hetty Hyssop, wiping her dripping nose. "My very dear Tom, you are an astonishingly brave person! How on earth could you stand

there as cool as a cucumber when she tore the veil off you? I don't believe it!"

"Oh well, you know," murmured Tom, embarrassed. "It could have been worse."

"Could have been worse?" cried Hetty Hyssop. "It was the most reckless, the most lunatic, and the bravest ghosthunting I've ever seen. My old heart almost packed it in. And then I went and fell in the moat as well. Talk about showing myself up!" Shaking her head, she looked down. "Oh well, that's nothing new. Perhaps I should give up this nerve-racking career and write my memoirs instead."

"What?" Tom sneezed violently. "Oh no, please don't. But couldn't we go into the warmth now? If my teeth chatter any longer, they'll fall out."

"Yes, of course!" cried Mr. Worm. "At once! Immediately! Though . . ." He cleared his throat, embarrassed. "Though I dropped the oars in the water with shock. I wonder if Mr. Hugo would be so kind as to pull us to shore?"

Hugo was so kind, and whilst Tom was warming himself up in front of the fire, Mrs. Worm set about preparing a bang-up breakfast in the castle kitchen.

Outside, a cold, gray morning was dawning, but it was cozy and warm in the enormous kitchen. It smelled of hot cocoa and toast, and Tom felt fantastic from his head down to the tips of his toes.

Just like heroes usually feel . . .

Then they all sat together at the big wooden table where the castle's servants once sat, eating French toast, fruit loaf with strawberry jam, and boiled eggs with toast. Yes, and Hugo once again told everyone how

Tom had offed the dreadful and totally moldy Baroness, doing a very good imitation of Jaspara's horrible voice. After all, the ASG had had a first-class view of events from his tree.

"I'll driiiink tooooo Toooom!" breathed Hugo, raising his glass. "The best ghost vaaaaaapooorizer ever!"

"Oh, stop it," murmured Tom, turning as red as a beet.

But Hugo hadn't finished.

"Aaaaand Iiiii'll drink," he continued, sipping some of the iced water that Mrs. Worm had given him, "Iiiii'll drink to the Baroness. She really was a viiiile, hideous ghost. And nooooo sense of humooooooor."

He giggled hollowly. "She just coooooouldn't take a joke, noooo, not at all."

"I wouldn't exactly find it funny if someone kept taking off my head," said Tom, spreading butter on his fourth piece of fruit loaf. Ghosthunting always left him starving.

"Noooo?" asked Hugo. "Iiiii doooon't believe it!"

And – *whisk!* – he had snatched Tom's glasses from his nose.

"Hugo," moaned Tom. "Stop that nonsense. Give me back my glasses."

"Nooo!" Hugo wobbled, giggling, up to the ceiling. "Not unless yoooou put that dress back on. Yoooou just look toooooo sweeeeet for words iiiin it."

"Mrs. Worm," said Tom, "could you possibly pass me a couple of raw eggs?"

"OK, OK," breathed Hugo, quickly wobbling back down. Like all ASGs, he was gripped by pure terror at the very sight of a raw egg. "Obviously yooooou have noooooo sense of humooooor, either." He sighed, putting Tom's glasses back on his nose. "That's a shame. A reeeal shame."

"Well, ghosts definitely have a very *weird* sense of humor," Tom replied, "and I confess I've had my fill of ghosts for today. No offense intended," he added to Hugo. "But I think I like the idea of Hyssop and Company having a few days' vacation."

"Well, we can't!" said Hetty Hyssop. "I've already accepted a job for next week. A **STKNOG** at a school. But Hugo and I can deal with that just as well on our own."

Tom realized he didn't like that idea at all. "No, no, that's fine," he said hastily. "STKNOGs are harmless. In any case I need one for my SGHD – Second GhostHunting Diploma."

"What – *hic* – is a STKNOG?" asked Mrs. Worm.

"A **ST**inking **KNO**cking **G**host," said Tom. "A pain, but harmless."

"And stuuuupid," breathed Hugo. "Terribly stuuupid."

Hetty Hyssop nodded. "Yes, pretty stupid. But I promise, my dear Tom, that we'll have two weeks' vacation afterward, OK?"

"OK," said Tom. Though he did wonder whether two weeks completely without ghosts might just be a bit boring after all. . . .

In Case of
an Encounter

Indeed, voracious readers, as your roving eyeballs have just witnessed in *Ghosthunters and the Totally Moldy Baroness!*, Tom barely managed to survive not only a death-defying drawbridge duel with a moth-eaten ghost but also the sheer humiliation of having to wear the old ghoul's dress in public. (As a sign of your utmost respect for your fellow ghosthunter, he politely requests that you not disclose this last fact, neither by blogging nor by text-messaging nor by cell-phoning.)

Naturally, it would never occur to you to pursue such a rotting apparition yourself, as the near-certain outcome of such a confrontation would be your dissolution into liquidized dirt that your intended prey would suck up like a filthy milk shake.

Howbeit . . .

In the exceptionally implausible instance of an unforeseen and utterly undesired interaction with a

HIGA – or with its even more malevolent subspecies, a GHADAP – or merely with an obstensibly innoxious, standard-issue, far-from-frightening apparition – the amateur ghosthunter is advised to subscribe to the following provisos:

PRECAUTIONARY MEASURES
against Ghosts in General

• The color red – as in socks, sweaters, curtains, sofas, and so on.

• Raw eggs, for throwing.

• Violet-scented perfume: Many species of ghost detest the smell. It makes their skin itch, and it has the added bonus of combating their natural and naturally foul ghost odor. For best results, spritz via an atomizer.

• Salt: It burns.

• Mirrors: Hang them on your red-painted walls; wear pocket-sized varieties when in the field.

- A spare pair of shoes: Depending on the variety of ghost, it will leave a trail that's sticky, snowy, muddy, etc. If in the thrill of the chase your sneakers get glued in place, it helps to have a backup.

- Graveyard dirt that's been gathered at night (*see* Ghosthunters and the Incredibly Revolting Ghost! *for specifics*).

- Chapels and crypts: With the exception of a few species, ghosts wouldn't be caught dead in these places; recommended as locations for regrouping when in the middle of a ghosthunt gone wrong.

- Daylight: Aim to accomplish the bulk of your ghosthunting during the day, as hauntings tend to intensify in the dark.

- Wind: A strong gust can blow a small-sized ghost to smithereens so, whenever possible, lure your prey into the eye of a storm.

- And no matter what, do not – do NOT – carry a flashlight on ghosthunting expeditions. The beam of a flashlight will drive a ghost into a violent rage.

- But don't bother whispering: Most ghosts can't hear very well, and rely instead on their sense of smell. (For this and reasons of basic human hygiene, ghosthunters should make a habit of bathing.)

IN CASE OF AN ENCOUNTER WITH A GIHUFO (Ghost In HUman FOrm)

- Fill a spray bottle with seawater — invaluable due to its inherent caustic saltiness — and carry at all times.

- Equip yourself with a seismograph specific to the species: It will register the ghost's impending approach with flashes and whirs.

- In advance of an anticipated attack, caulk the cracks around windowsills and door frames with mint toothpaste; this will keep a GIHUFO from creeping through.

- Suck on an antidotal lozenge: The good news is the utterly vile flavor repulses even the most determined body-nabber. The bad news is the utterly vile flavor.

- In the absence of aforementioned repulsive lozenge, bite your tongue!

TO CATCH A TIBIG
(TIny BIting Ghost)

- Set a trap of sticky paper strips that stink of mouse droppings (*see Hyssop & Co.'s mail-order catalog for precut one-, three-, and five-foot lengths; the assorted-length multipack; and the 8-roll Stinky Strip® cut-your-own refills with value-added bonus bag of fresh mouse droppings*).

- Transport the stuck TIBIGs in a fine-meshed net.

TO COMBAT A HIGA
(HIstorical Ghostly Apparition)

- Verify the HIGA's time, date, and place of death — as well as how it died — at the earliest opportunity possible: To vanquish the ghost, key aspects of its original death have to be reenacted. A Spooky Energy Visualizer is suggested to ascertain the exact location of the ghost's death.

- To that end, safeguard books, biographical records, and other relevant arcana, as the HIGA will attempt to destroy any documentation of its human existence — and demise.

• Preemptively cut off all power supplies. Flip the switch on the fuse box; shut down and/or dispose of any batteries or generators within the vicinity of the haunting. If time does not permit for their disposal, neutralize by dousing with anti-HIGA solution.

• Employ a Heat-Intensifying Device: Admittedly, this device requires a certain amount of skill to use; amateur ghosthunters may find the dual actions of anchoring the spike while roping the HIGA with the conductive plug a tad challenging. But when successfully employed, a HID draws power away from battery-charged ghosts and transforms it into heat – which, of course, almost all ghosts hate.

• Unleash a TIBIG or two (*see previous section*): Less technologically advanced than the HID but impressively effective, TIBIGs will set about cannibalizing larger ghosts, including HIGAs, by biting huge chunks out of useful body parts. Although the holey ghosts can eventually regenerate themselves, it is a slow, energy-consuming process – one that buys valuable time for besieged ghosthunters.

WHAT TO EXPECT IF YOU'RE
POSSESSED BY A GHADAP
(GHost With A DArk Past; subspecies of HIGA)

• Repellent giggling.

• Pumpkinheaditis: The head of the possessed will
light up like a jack-o'-lantern; the facial features will
blur as if made of liquid; the eyebrows will thicken
unflatteringly; the hair will drip green slime.

• A residual puddle, greenish gray in color, muddy in
consistency.

• Temporary mental confusion.

• Twenty-four hours of hiccups.

IN CASE OF AN ENCOUNTER WITH
A GHADAP

• An itchy, tingling sensation is a typical response to
a GHADAP's touch. If you feel anything other than,
and/or above and beyond, tingled – or if you are

otherwise ill-equipped for a counterattack – run.
Run away as fast as you can. In a zigzag pattern.
(*Note: Marathon zigzaggers recommend fixing your
vision on a distant focal point so as to avoid (a) making
yourself dizzy to the point of passing out; and
(b) accidentally zigzagging back toward the ghost you
are attempting to flee.*)

• Don rubber boots and gloves: These counter
mudpuddlication (that is, the transformation of the
victim into a puddle of mud), thereby delaying
the GHADAP's opportunity to slurp up your muddy
remains.

• Uncover a personal item from the ghost's human
past, then trick the GHADAP into touching it. *Poof!*
The ghost goes up in smoke – or, more accurately,
mist. Recommended past-life items include: old bed
linens; worn-out stockings and socks; suits of
armors; royal gowns; riding britches; and soiled
handkerchiefs.

• Alternately, write the ghost's human name backward
on a mirror, then get the GHADAP to gaze at its
reflection. *Poof!* etc.

Indispensable Alphabetical
APPENDIX OF ASSORTED GHOSTS

AG	**A**ncient **G**host
ASG	**A**veragely **S**pooky **G**host
BLAGDO	**BLA**ck **G**host **DO**g
BOSG	**BO**g and **S**wamp **G**host
CAG	**CA**stle **G**host
CG	**C**ellar **G**host
COHAG	**CO**mpletely **HA**rmless **G**host
FG	**F**ire **G**host
FOFIFO	**FO**ggy **FI**gure **FO**rmer
FOFUG	**FO**ggy **FU**g-**G**host
GG	**G**raveyard **G**host
GHADAP	**GH**ost with **A DA**rk **P**ast
GIHUFO	**G**host **I**n **HU**man **FO**rm
GILIG	**G**ruesome **I**nvincible **LI**ghtning **G**host
HIGA	**HI**storical **G**hostly **A**pparition
IRG	**I**ncredibly **R**evolting **G**host

MG	**M**arsh **G**host
MUWAG	**MU**ddy **WA**ters **G**host
NEPGA	**NE**gative **P**rojection of a **G**hostly **A**pparition
PAWOG	**PA**le **WO**bbly **G**host
STKNOG	**ST**inking **KNO**cking **G**host
TIBIG	**TI**ny **BI**ting **G**host
TOHAG	**TO**tally **HA**rmless **G**host
TOMOB	**TO**tally **MO**ldy **B**aroness
WG	**W**ater **G**host
WHIWHI	**WHI**rlwind **WHI**rler

Miscellaneous Listing of
NECESSITOUS EQUIPMENT AND
NOTEWORTHY ORGANIZATIONS

CDEGH   Clinic for the **DE**-spookification of **G**host**H**unters

CECOCOG   **CE**ntral **CO**mmission for **CO**mbating **G**hosts

COCOT   **CO**ntact-**CO**mpression **T**rap

FIGHD   **FI**fth **G**host**H**unting **D**iploma

GES   **G**hostly **E**nergy **S**ensor

GHOSID   **GHO**st-**SI**mulation **D**isguise

HID   **H**eat-**I**ntensifying **D**evice

LOAG   **L**ist **O**f **A**ll Known **G**hosts

NENEB   **NE**gative-**NE**utralizer **B**elt

OFFCOCAG   **OFF**ice for **CO**mbating **CA**stle **G**hosts

RCFCAG   **R**etention **C**enter **F**or **C**riminally **A**ggressive **G**hosts

RICOG   **R**esearch **I**nstitute for **CO**mbating **G**hosts

ROGA	**R**egister **O**ffice for **G**hostly **A**pparitions
SEV	**S**pook **E**nergy **V**isualizer
SGHD	**S**econd **G**host**H**unting **D**iploma
THGHD	**TH**ird **G**host**H**unting **D**iploma

A Daring Plan

It took Hetty Hyssop and Tom nearly a quarter of an hour to convince the inhabitants of Bogpool that their village had turned into one of the most dangerous places on Earth. Packed together like sardines, most of them still in bathrobes and pajamas, the villagers sat listening, their faces ashen with horror, to Tom's description of the Zargoroth. Only the vicar's sister interrupted Tom several times to call out that she'd said so all along. When Hetty Hyssop told them how deadly the Thirteenth Messenger was, switching the lights off as she ended her speech, there was no way the Bogpoolers were staying in their seats any longer.

Ten minutes later, Tom, Hetty Hyssop, and Erwin Hornheaver were standing alone in the dark hall, surrounded by nothing but overturned chairs and lost bedroom slippers.

"Well, Hornheaver," said Hetty Hyssop. "Pack whatever you want to save from the mud and get yourself to safety."

But Erwin Hornheaver didn't stir. He stared blackly at the gurgling mud that was flowing through the open front door and into the playground. "And what are you two going to do now, may I ask?"

"Well, we'll try to prepare a nice welcome for the Zargoroth," replied Tom.

Erwin Hornheaver nodded and surveyed the upturned chairs. "Reckon you two could use a bit of help, couldn't you?"

Tom and Hetty Hyssop exchanged surprised looks.

"Y'know," Hornheaver continued, "I've never been very afraid of these ghosts. I was a boxer once upon a time, before I inherited my aunt's inn, and I only give up if I'm knocked out. If you get my drift."

"That really is a very generous offer, Hornheaver," said Hetty Hyssop. "And I hope you've got some idea of what you're getting yourself into. Tom, have we got a third pair of protective goggles with us?"

Tom rummaged around in his backpack. "I haven't

got any on me," he said finally. "But I think there's a spare in the suitcase."

"Good." Hetty Hyssop nodded and gave Erwin Hornheaver an appreciative thump on the shoulders. "It's not often that someone offers to help us," she said. "And tonight's a night when we'd really appreciate it, isn't it, Tom?"

"Too right," murmured Tom, who was disconcerted to see that the mud was flowing faster and faster into the school.

It was now twenty to three. The night was still young. And they didn't have the faintest idea how they were to fight whatever was coming for them.

By twenty after three, Bogpool was a deserted village. Erwin Hornheaver had walked around the place and hadn't encountered a single living being. Not even a cat or a hen. The Bogpoolers had taken their livestock and horses with them. And mud and fog were taking possession of one house after another.

"Good!" said Hetty Hyssop, pacing energetically up and down their room. "Everyone's gone, so we can get to work. How are you getting on, Tom?"

123

"Still nothing," Tom spat through clenched teeth. Ever since they'd gotten back from the assembly hall, he'd been crouching in front of the computer, typing in one keyword after another – in the desperate hope of turning up some clue as to how they were supposed to fight the Zargoroth. Tom's eyes hurt, and he had to keep taking his glasses off to rub away the veil of tiredness that made the words on the screen swim around in front of him. "Nothing," he said, and shook his head. "We just don't know enough about this ghost. It's enough to drive you crazy."

"That **NE**gative **P**rojection of a **G**hostly **A**pparition isn't talking, eeeeeeeeeeither!" breathed Hugo, tapping the **CO**ntact **CO**mpression **T**rap with his finger. "Iiiii've triiiiiied reeeeeeeally hard tooooo persuaaaaaade him, ghoooooost to ghooooooost, but Iiiii can't get a peeeeeeep ooout of him. Conceeeeited frazzled idiiiiiiot ghoooost!"

Tom sat bolt upright.

"What?" Both Hugo and Hetty Hyssop looked at him.

"That's it!" Tom cried, snapping the computer shut. "That's our only chance!"

"Does he often speak in riddles?" growled

Hornheaver, giving Hetty Hyssop a mug of hot coffee and Tom his fourth can of soda.

"Hugo, put the **COCOT** under my pillow," said Tom, "so the **NEPGA** can't hear what we're talking about."

The ASG did as he was told, and Tom lowered his voice.

"There's only one thing to do!" he whispered. "We let the NEPGA go, then follow it to its master. Once we've actually set eyes on the Zargoroth, we might be able to identify what kind of ghost that is — and how we can fight it!"

Tom felt really pleased with himself and his idea, but Hetty Hyssop frowned. "That's a dangerous idea, my dear boy," she said. "Even if I were to agree to such a plan, how do you propose to follow a NEPGA? Human legs are definitely too slow, and what are you going to do if it flies? Or if it just floats through a wall?"

"We could coat it in a mixture of baking powder and scouring sand," replied Tom. "That slows ghosts down and stops them from going through walls. And as far as flying is concerned, you know I'm really not that keen on it, but . . ." He turned to Hugo and didn't finish his sentence.

The ASG turned the color of pale mold. "Ooooooh! What's that looooook suuuuupposed to meeeeeean?"

"You can carry me on your back!" said Tom. "In all that fog out there, you're as good as invisible, but you can see the NEPGA as clearly as anything. We can follow it to its master, find out exactly what we're dealing with – and then fly back here. Not very difficult, is it?"

"Ha! Ha-haaaaa!" Hugo rolled his garish green eyes. "Not veeery difficult, heeeeee says!"

"You ought to let Hugo do it on his own, Tom," said Hetty Hyssop. "The job isn't half as dangerous for a ghost as it is for a human."

"Pah, it's dangerous eeeeenoooooough!" grumbled Hugo – but Hetty Hyssop gave him such a fierce look that he shut up.

"He can't do it on his own!" cried Tom. "He doesn't know anything about identifying and classifying ghosts. I bet Hugo can recognize at most five percent of them!"

"At mosssssst!" breathed Hugo, showing his agreement by banging Tom on the back.

Hetty Hyssop shook her head. "I don't like this," she said. "No. There has to be another way. After all, the Ghost of Death's spooking around out there as well."

"Oh, I've got the protective goggles," said Tom dismissively. "That really isn't a problem."

Erwin Hornheaver hadn't spoken thus far. But now he cleared his throat. "Leave the boy alone!" he told Hetty Hyssop, topping up her coffee mug. "He can do it. You told me yourself what a first-class ghost-hunter he is."

Tom was thankful for this unexpected support, but Hetty Hyssop looked at him and sighed. "Well, yes, he certainly is!" she said. "He's one of the best, one of the very best."

Tom turned as red as tomato juice.

"That settles it, then," he said, self-consciously setting his glasses straight. "Have you got any baking powder and scouring sand, Mr. Hornheaver?"

"Erwin," growled Erwin Hornheaver. "My name is Erwin, lad, and I think I've got both."

This was Tom's plan: Hugo was to play with the COCOT until the trap – oops, what a shame! – released itself, whereupon he was to throw it out the window in horror. There, Tom would already be waiting with the full sprinkler and would bombard the NEPGA with baking powder and scouring sand as soon as it freed itself from the trap.

"I just hope Hugo doesn't mess it all up!" whispered Tom as he and Hetty Hyssop stood below in the foggy street. The white haze was so thick by now that Tom could hardly make out their bedroom window. He himself was barely visible, either. He was wearing what's known in ghosthunting circles as a **GHOSID** (**GHO**st-**SI**mulation **D**isguise): pale, moldy green overalls with a hood and gloves of the same color; and his face was covered in almost a pound of makeup that went by the name of "Ghostly Pallor." On top of that, he was surrounded by a faint smell of cellars, as the smaller, harmless ghosts often are. Tom, unfortunately, hadn't been able to change anything about his body temperature, but it was entirely possible for some ghosts to radiate something very similar to human warmth.

There was just one more problem, and it worried Hetty Hyssop more than anything else: Tom needed to wear the goggles to protect himself from being looked at by the Ghost of Death – but he was supposed to be disguised as a ghost, and no real ghost would wear such a thing. Tom, however, promised to have them always on hand and to put them on as soon as he and Hugo were on their way back. Thankfully, his normal glasses wouldn't give him away.

Wearing glasses is not unusual in the ghostly world.

Tom pulled the moldy green hood down even more tightly over his forehead. The village, devoid of humans, was ghostly silent; only the stones were still moaning and the mud gurgling – and Hugo's voice resounded clearly down to them through the milky darkness.

"Soooooo, it's maaaaaaking yoooooou dizzzzzy, yoooooooou shaaaaady character, is it?" Tom could hear him howling. "Cooooooome on. What's it liiiiiiike in there, my liiiiittle goooooooldfish?"

"Ten more seconds," whispered Hetty Hyssop, not taking her eyes off her illuminated wristwatch. "Nine, eight, seven . . ."

"Yoooooou'll looooooook great in the muuuuuuuuseum for captuuuuured ghooooosts!" breathed Hugo. "A reeeeeeal jewel in ooooooour cooooooollection."

"Three!" whispered Hetty Hyssop. "Two, one, and – zero!"

Holding their breath, they looked up at the fog-shrouded window. "Come on, Hugo!" whispered

Tom, holding the full sprinkler. At that very moment, it happened.

The COCOT flew through the air . . . and landed in a lake of mud.

"Curses!" hissed Tom. "It's sinking. What now?"

But the NEPGA was already arising from the mud. Dripping, it raised itself from the swamp like the shadow of a dark dream.

This was Tom's moment. With one leap, he bounded into the street, sank up to his knees in the brown goo – and raised the sprinkler.

"Yooooooou!" breathed the NEPGA, floating threateningly over to him. "Yoooooooou dared . . ."

"Not one foot farther!" cried Tom, sprinkling Erwin Hornheaver's entire supply of baking powder and scouring sand onto its dark body. The NEPGA coughed and tried with smoky gray fingers to wipe the burning powder off its body, but Tom knew it wouldn't succeed. With an angry screech the ghost flew up into the sky – and disappeared into the swirling fog.

"Hugo!" cried Tom, casting aside the empty sprinkler. "Hugo, where are you?"

But the ASG was already floating out the window.

He was barely visible in the fog. With icy fingers, he lifted Tom up onto his shoulders.

"Don't take any risks, Tom!" cried Hetty Hyssop. "Remember the Thirteenth Messenger and don't, whatever you do, try to fight the Zargoroth on your own!"

But Tom and Hugo had already been swallowed up by the fog.